Madeline L

Gender Theory

Fiona,

M. Darby

Xo

JOHN MURRAY

First published in Great Britain in 2024 by John Murray (Publishers)

I

Copyright © Madeline Docherty 2024

The right of Madeline Docherty to be identified as the
Author of the Work has been asserted by her in accordance
with the Copyright, Designs and Patents Act 1988.

A CIP catalogue record for this title is available from the British Library

Hardback ISBN 9781399812184
Trade Paperback ISBN 9781399812191
ebook ISBN 9781399812214

Typeset in Sabon MT by Hewer Text UK Ltd, Edinburgh
Printed and bound in Great Britain by Clays Ltd, Elcograf S.p.A.

John Murray policy is to use papers that are natural, renewable and
recyclable products and made from wood grown in sustainable forests.
The logging and manufacturing processes are expected to conform
to the environmental regulations of the country of origin.

Carmelite House
50 Victoria Embankment
London EC4Y 0DZ

www.johnmurraypress.co.uk

John Murray Press, part of Hodder & Stoughton Limited
An Hachette UK company

To Ellen – my partner in wine, my karaoke companion, my first editor, my best friend.

I wanted so badly to escape my skin, but I couldn't. I couldn't get out and nobody could get in. The boundaries of the body are non-negotiable.

Lucia Osborne-Crowley

Student Halls

You are eighteen and this is the first time you have voiced desire, asked for something that you wanted, and received it. He is a year older than you, tall, intellectual, more experienced. You have been sitting cross-legged on his bed for an hour, talking about films, him seemingly unaware of you leaning forward, biting your lip, doing all of the things you're supposed to. Your responses become shorter and shorter as your conversation becomes his monologue about strong women in film. He's just started telling you about The Bride in *Kill Bill*, when you put your hands on his upper arms and kiss him.

Soon, you are sitting on his lap, trying to get lost but worrying about how heavy you are, hoping your foundation won't come off on his sheets. His arms are thin and sinewy, and he has wrapped them around you tight. You are trying to ignore the damp smell of his room, and the fact that there was nowhere to hang your coat so it's just lying crumpled on the floor next to a plate with crumbs on it. The kissing is a beginning, so both of your movements are sloppy and hurried. He pulls his T-shirt over his head and it gets stuck on his earring and at the same time you notice that he hasn't got any curtains so the moonlight streams into the room from behind his body. It silhouettes his frame inside the T-shirt as he struggles, and you start to laugh but you are cut off when he frees himself and puts his mouth back onto yours.

For a few moments there is no noise except wet, sucking mouths and tongues. But then your moans are in conversation, his first, then yours in reply. Soon after, too soon really, he is thrusting into you in the way a broken gutter smacks against a building. You are on your back looking at his face and his gaze is angled downward at your chest. You lower yours and look at his collarbones and ribs, visible underneath his pale skin. You think about butterflies wearing their skeleton on the outside of their papery wings. You breathe deeply because it has started to hurt, but not enough to say anything and engage in the necessary reassembling of parts. The metal bed frame starts creaking and a minute later his eyes close as he cries out and sort of sinks onto you, his hard body biting your soft one. Did you? he asks and you reply, yeah, yeah. You clean up and dress and he stays in bed, covers pulled up to his belly button, clicking on and off videos on his phone. The small bursts of noise keep making you jump as they fill the room, and you are trying not to look at him while you put on your socks. Dressing feels more vulnerable than being naked, somehow, and you can see him sneaking glances at you from the mirror on his chest of drawers.

You walk over to the bed and lean in to kiss him, like an ending this time, and he says, will you still come out on Thursday? And you say, of course! even though this is the first time he's asked you. Then you walk out of his room, across the hallway, out the door and down the stairs, spilling into the moonlight and taking your phone out of your coat pocket. You have a series of texts from Ella, asking where you are, when you're coming home and then: wait. are you with seminar boy??? You start walking back to halls, which is home now, and every few steps you close your eyes and take a deep breath in, feeling the cold air on your face. You realise that you're lost as the streets begin to blur into each other. You want to stop and check your phone, get your bearings, but the night is so quiet you force yourself to keep going so you can reassure yourself with the sound of your boots hitting pavement.

You feel like this city could be yours sometimes, when it opens itself up to you and gives you things you were longing for before you came here; gay bars, vintage shops, night buses, boys that read gender theory. But tonight, in the dark, it is turning away from you, reminding you that you don't know these streets yet, that you can't zone out and let your feet take you home safely. For the first time since you left, you miss the downhill slope of the high street in the village you grew up in, the way you used to cycle home from parties, pedals still as you flew, helmetless and drunk from contraband booze. The stakes feel different now, with no parents to enforce curfews and a new home that's more than five minutes away. But you keep walking and after a few minutes, miraculously, you stumble onto your street, and recognise the flats, and the light is on at the student support office. You can hear the music from several different parties going on in several different flats, all full of freshers like you at the very beginning of growing up. As you walk into your hallway, Ella comes out of her room, grinning, and leads you into the kitchen. You know your night won't be real until you share it with her. She puts the kettle on, and you tell her everything.

Flat Parties

You are drunk and you can't find Ella, and you're talking to someone who is definitely on coke because they aren't leaving gaps in their speech long enough for you to answer them. And they aren't asking questions anyway, they're just talking talking talking and their words melt away and turn into a rhythm in your head that matches the music, which also has no words so you're just kind of swaying to the thumping of the talking and the music and your head, which has started hurting because you've stayed at this party way too long. You float out of yourself and start wondering how you look to other people, if anyone here finds you attractive, if anyone has tapped their friend on the shoulder at any point in the night and said, hey who's that? and then Ella taps you on the shoulder and you spin around and think oh, there she is. And she is drunk too, but not as drunk as you, and her eyes are sparkly and wet like she's been crying or laughing really hard. And she grabs your arm and steers you out of the conversation and you go and sit in the kitchen to smoke. You perch yourself on the worktop and ash into the sink and start making fun of your surroundings. You ask her if she's noticed that now everyone you know has moved into real flats, they've all been attempting grown-up decor; plants, reusable coffee cups, shoe racks, but they also can't escape the tacky accessories of student living; a pyramid made of beer cans, a traffic cone, a cardboard cut-out of an ironic celebrity (in this case, Danny DeVito), a wall of Polaroids. She's laughing now, which makes you laugh too, and when someone comes into the kitchen and asks what you're laughing at, you both just laugh harder. And the best part of the joke is that your flat is exactly the same – you even have a record player and a drawer specifically for tote bags – and you love all of the clichés about art students because they're true, and it makes you feel like you are part of something. You try to explain this to her, but you're drunk, so you just trail off halfway through a sentence and say . . . you know? And she says, yeah definitely. And then you ask if she wants to go, and she does, so you split up and start making your separate ways around the flat, collecting coat, bag, shoes and saying good-bye to everyone. You meet her at the door and, as you open it, you can't believe the sun is rising. And she grabs you and says, I forgot, it's the summer solstice. And you link arms and start walking and you're both silent, looking at the pink and orange dawn sky, and you're thinking about how warm she is, how you can feel the heat of her skin through her thin sleeves. And you are thinking about how comfortable silence is with her, how there are no empty words or misjudgements. And you are struggling to keep hidden that hot ball of feelings that lives in the bottom of your gut and comes out on night/mornings like this, the one that's made up of curves and sweet-smelling hair and girl-on-girl searches and aborted touching. And a question is rolling around your drunk brain and you wonder if you'll ever be able to ask it. And you look at her and think, she was the prettiest girl at the party, at any party, anywhere.

*

Your devil horns are digging into the sides of your head, so you take them off and set them on a table covered with half-empty bottles of mixer, shot glasses and packets of tobacco. A boy in your Victorian Lit seminar invited you to this party and the theme is heaven and hell and the second you walked in someone wearing a nun costume asked if you wanted to do poppers. You move into the kitchen to look for your stashed Lambrini and get into a conversation with a girl dressed as an angel. She says, how's hell? And you say, hot, and she laughs. You can't find your booze, but she pours you a vodka coke and asks where she knows you from. You say you don't know, and she tugs your tutu and says, gay? And you say, um? And she pulls up her dress and asks if you like her suspenders. You make an excuse and leave and keep looking for Ella, but instead you walk head first into two girls fighting over a phone, the taller of the two holding it high above her head and shouting, no fucking way! You make eye contact with her, and she says meaningfully, she's trying to text her ex. You nod in understanding.

You feel out of place; you are wearing too many clothes, there's no glitter on your face, you're too shy to walk up to somebody and start a conversation. You realise that when you do find Ella, she is probably going to be charming a crowd, making people laugh and feel at ease, the way she does with everyone – the way she did with you. You drain your drink and go back into the kitchen and find the angel. She asks if you want another, and you say yes. She apologises for being full on – I thought I had seen you at the LGBT+ nights – and asks if you can start again. You are impressed by her effortless retreat from flirting to friendship, and curious as to whether she has seen something in you that you are still uncovering. She introduces herself; you aren't sure if she says Katie or Kasey, and you talk about your classes, how you're finding second year, where you're from. She's excited to go home for Christmas, you aren't, the conversation is filler, but you're hanging on her every word. After your third vodka coke you ask if she wants to go outside for a cigarette. She grabs your hand to pull you through the hallway, which is now full of bodies and vibrating with bass, you open the door into the close and make your way down the stairs. She doesn't let go of your hand until you are out of the building. You sit on the steps leading up to the flat and she lights two cigarettes in her mouth and gives one to you. You take a draw, exhale, wait a moment.

I think I am, you say, before you can talk yourself out of it.

You think you're what?

Gay, or bi, I guess. I do like boys.

She laughs and says that she likes boys too. That she likes everyone. You feel more confident now you've said it out loud. She asks you if you've kissed girls before and you shake your head. She asks if you want to, and you nod. When she leans in and puts her lips on yours, she is gentle. You feel drunk and happy, and you want to keep kissing forever. When she pulls away, she is wearing your lipstick. You want her to leave it like that all night, smudged around her mouth, you want everybody to know that you put it there. You are smiling, a little stupidly, and she laughs at you and says,

No longer a hypothetical bisexual.

No.

At that moment, a group of girls burst through the door, led by Ella, and she almost trips over you. She is sweaty, like she's been dancing, and she is clutching a packet of cigarettes. She holds them up to you triumphantly and exclaims, I stole these! She sits in between you and the angel, and the other girls surround you on the lower steps. You stay out there for an hour or more, chatting, enjoying the cool air and the absence of techno music. Somebody has found your bottle of Lambrini, and you pass it around taking swigs of warm, sugary liquid. One of the girls knows the angel and elbows her and says,

I should have known you would be out here seducing people. You've got lipstick all over your face.

The angel shrugs and says, what can I say, I can always spot the best-looking girl at the party, and Ella looks at her and then back at you. She points at your face, which is probably also a mess of lipstick, and makes an exaggerated 'O' with her mouth. She leans in and whispers to you,

Interesting development.

And you reply,

I know, right?

*

You are having a party to celebrate the end of the summer term. It is the first time you have had people over to the flat properly, despite living here almost a year, and you want the evening to be more refined than your usual fare. You get the bus to IKEA and buy eight plates, extra cutlery, some real cocktail glasses. You decide on an Italian theme, do a test run of the food the weekend before, but the pasta keeps coming out too thick, because you don't have an actual pasta maker. You pivot to fajitas. You make a Facebook event with the updated theme and write: think more chic Mexican dinner party and less depraved student sesh. You spend the last of your loan on mid-price tequila and all the limes in the local supermarket. The cashier asks you sarcastically if you have enough and Ella replies, deadpan, no.

The night is a failure from the beginning. Everyone you invited brings at least three extra people, and most of them are drunk. The frozen margaritas take too long to make, so people start shotting the tequila instead. You keep asking if anyone is ready to eat, but nobody will sit down, and they're filling up on the snacks anyway, crushing crisps into your carpet and dropping globs of guacamole on the furniture. Ella hisses in your ear, I cannot believe I bought a fucking mortar and pestle for *this*. You become almost hysterical with laughter, watching people you vaguely know from lectures and seminars yell at each other and take shots and disappear to the bathroom for long stretches, returning with dilated pupils and nervous tics. At half eleven, everybody leaves to get taxis into town and go out, and you survey the carnage. The two of you begin to tidy up half-heartedly, you in the living room and Ella in the kitchen. After a few minutes, you hear the whizz of the blender, and then Ella comes in with a jug of frozen margarita, glasses and straws. You put on the playlist you made for the evening and dance around the room, racing each other to the bottom of your glasses. A few hours later, you have eaten the fajitas, used an impressive number of the limes, and are lying on your living room carpet, which is still sticky, laughing at the catastrophe of your first dinner party. Ella says, one day we'll do it properly, when our peers are as mature and sophisticated as we are. You laugh, because the drunker you get, the funnier Ella is, and say, okay it's a deal.

Glasgow Royal Infirmary

You have to leave the library because your stomach starts cramping, pain washing over you in waves, something inside of you tensing and releasing. You've come off the pill and for the past few months your period has felt like a punishment. You feel something slide out of you and think, blood. You shove your laptop in your bag, banging it against the table and someone opposite you starts and looks up, annoyed. As you make your way down the stairs you have to stop for a second, clutch the bannister and take deep breaths. Your jumper is stuck to your wet back and your scarf is half-falling out of your bag and dragging on the ground. With every swell of pain your vision shimmers. You make it outside and collapse onto a bench, your senses shocked by the dark and the cold. You forget what time it is, how long you've been in the library, when you last ate, thoughts pushed from your head by the pain. You take your phone out of your pocket, pause when you get to your mum's contact. You call her and listen to the phone ring once, twice, three times, before you realise that you don't know what you would say if she answered. You hang up and call Ella. When you hear her voice you realise you're holding back tears. You have to come and get me, you say, your own voice sounding far away from you, like you're shouting to yourself from across the road. Fifteen minutes later she's stumbling out of a taxi and helping you straight back in.

You wait in A&E for hours, surrounded by drunk people and crying babies, your head on her shoulder, your hand in hers, and when someone finally calls your name, you snap out of a doze. Ella asks if you want her to come and see the doctor with you and you shake your head and leave her sitting on a plastic seat, pulling a copy of *Little Women* out of her bag as you are led down a hall that smells like alcohol and piss. The doctor is male, and young, and when you start to tell him your medical history he flinches almost imperceptibly at the words 'period' and 'painful sex'. He asks if you've tried taking ibuprofen and putting a hot water bottle on your stomach for the cramps. He sounds bored. You wish then that she was here with you, to make sure you don't forget anything, to keep holding your hand. You've been meaning to schedule an appointment, but you were worried about something like this happening, about your words coming out stupid, about being the girl complaining about something her body was made to do.

Another wave hits and you say, oh my god I'm going to be sick, and the doctor grabs a bedpan and brings it up to your face in one smooth motion. You throw up noisily and untidily, splashing his sleeve a little, vomit coming out of your nose in a hot, stinging stream. You can feel more blood seeping out of you and staining the paper sheet on the hospital bed. When you stop throwing up you lie back on the bed with your eyes closed, too spent to feel embarrassed, and the doctor says, gently this time, are you okay? The room is quiet, except for the whirring of the computer. And then you say, I don't know. He decides to keep you in overnight and tells you that someone will come and give you painkillers and iron tablets in the morning. He also books you in for a gynaecological scan and tells you that you're lucky to get such a quick appointment. The date on the piece of paper he gives you is four months away. You can't stop looking at your vomit on his cuff. Soon after, a young nurse shows you to a bed on a busy ward full of old people with swollen ankles and thin hair. You are given a flimsy pair of hospital pyjamas and a cup of watery tea.

Ella comes to see you to say goodbye and when she bends over to hug you, you say, stay? For a few minutes. Until they kick you out. She pulls the curtain around your section and sits on the chair beside your bed. You ask, what bit of *Little Women* are you at? And she says, shall I read it? And she starts to read and you close your eyes to listen to her voice, and you know that usually you would start arguing about who was Jo and who was Amy right now, but you can't focus your thoughts enough to get the words out, so you just pretend that you're at home fighting, and that soon you're going to open a bottle of wine and pretend you won't drink it all. And a bit later you'll dance in the kitchen like in *Practical Magic*, and your body will feel strong and unchanged in the light of the fridge. You wake up a few hours later when a nurse checks your blood pressure and feel Ella's absence in the darkness as the band of the machine tightens around your upper arm.

7 University Gardens

You drop your takeaway coffee in the doorway of the seminar room and the word fuck! escapes from your mouth before you can stop it. You look up and the room is full because you are a few minutes late, and everyone is looking at you. There are a few chairs stacked in the corner and hardly any space left for you to sit. At the head of the table is, you assume, your tutor. He's handsome but he's wearing awful glasses, like the fake ones that come with a moustache and eyebrows. His clothes and face tell you that he was privately educated. He is still wearing his raincoat and the comedy glasses are a little bit steamed up, like he was late too. He jumps up and hurries over to help you, pulling tissues out of his pocket and saying no harm done! I hate that carpet anyway.

Everyone laughs and stops looking at you, busying themselves by pulling laptops and notebooks out of bags. He crouches down and so do you, both of you dabbing ineffectually at the stain. You say, oh my god I am so sorry, and he says, seriously, it's fine. After a minute you both give up and he sits back down while you unstack one of the chairs and squeeze yourself into a corner. He talks about the course then, checks that everyone has bought the primary texts, asks if anybody has a personal interest in Romantic poetry. The only other boy in the room puts his hand up and your tutor smiles at him, then laughs and says, tough crowd, that's okay, I know this is a course requirement. He says that he is a year into a PhD, that this is his second ever under-grad class, and his favourite fruit is mango. You all have to introduce yourselves then and say your favourite fruit. It's excruciating. When it is your turn, you say you love straw-berries and he smiles and says, like the Edwin Morgan poem? You know he used to teach here. And you smile back at him and say, yeah, I know.

Three weeks later, he is kissing you for the first time; in his office, against the wall, and you are so turned on your legs are shaking. He keeps saying is this alright, are you okay? against your mouth, stammering like a schoolboy. You nod your head and kiss him back. You have been emailing back and forth since the first class, ignoring Ella, who uses every chance she gets to tell you it's a cliché and you're in over your head. You know that she's right, but the emails break up the mundanity of your daily routine, give you something to think about that isn't your health. You're trying a new contraceptive pill that makes you shout and cry and bloats your stomach out like a balloon. You've been running the packets together to skip your periods and so far, it's been working. You aren't in physical pain anymore, but your moods have become unpredictable and hard to endure.

He doesn't know about your broken body or your unstable moods. You don't talk about your lives, your friends, the day-to-day. You talk about language and dead poets and his dreams of being a writer. You know almost nothing concrete about him, but when he touches you, you forget your own name. He pulls away from your kiss and smiles at you, all white teeth and glowing eyes, and for a second you go cold but you aren't sure why. Then he kisses you again and you're lost, pulling him closer until your bodies are pressed together, you on your tiptoes, him stooping down a little. He starts kissing your ear, then your neck, and then he groans and whispers to you, *her hair was long*, and he tugs the end of your ponytail and whispers again, *her eyes were wild*, and he kisses the side of your eyelids, and murmurs, *I made a garland for your head*, and he strokes your face and you hear Ella's voice in your head say come *on*, but you shake it off and make your eyes wide and look up at him again, like you're turning your face up to the sun.

As you walk home you keep crossing the road without looking because you are thinking about the smooth skin at the back of his neck. You watch your reflection in shop windows and your face is red with cold and the memory of the kissing. Your mum texts you saying, not heard from you in a while? and you start to reply but then he emails you. The subject line says, I cannot stop, and the body of the email reads, thinking about you. You fall in love with how the email makes you feel, like something desirable, like something worth pursuing. Impulsively, you cancel your gynaecology appointment, thinking you could live like this forever, running pill packets together and never knowing what was wrong. When you get home Ella is watering your dead plants but when she sees you, she abandons the task and starts making tea. She adds almond milk and honey without asking and you take the steaming mugs into your scabby garden to smoke. You sit in silence for a minute, and she stretches her arms above her head and yawns, her jumper riding up so you can see her soft stomach. Then she looks at you innocently and says,

So, how was your sex meeting then?
and you roll your eyes and say, we didn't have sex.
She stares at you.
But we did kiss.
She keeps staring.
And he quoted a poem to me.
She purses her lips,
What poem? No wait actually let me guess, Bukowski?
You shake your head.
E.E. Cummings?
You shake your head again. She thinks for a second,
Keats?
You start to laugh, and Ella puts her head in her hands and groans. You keep laughing and the noise frightens a crow picking at the rubbish bins. She points at the dark shape flying away and says, bad omen, and then she starts laughing too and the spell is broken.

When you see him in seminars, you communicate in code. When someone delivers a particularly stupid answer, he raises an eyebrow, just for you. You never put your hand up, and only speak once or twice a class, but when you do, you try your best to share astute observations on the text, or to make a joke about one of the poets. You wear his laughter like a badge of honour, his approval sustaining you during the weeks where you cannot meet privately. You do the seminar reading every week, sometimes twice, trying to fake a natural intellect that you don't have, trying to love the things that he loves. You read beyond the compulsory theory, seeking out journal articles and essays analysing the work. They seem to be written in a different language, and you are too afraid to ask anyone else what they mean, afraid of being laughed at. You join the poetry society and sit at the edge of con-versations, pretending to be au fait with the vocabulary, using words like syntax and enjambment. You listen carefully and copy down the opinions of the smartest people in the group, transcribing their observations word for word in your emails to him. When he replies quickly and compliments your remarks, you glow. When he doesn't reply for days, or sends you a few distracted lines, the circles under your eyes darken into bruises.

Once that semester, he takes one of your lectures, and you spend two hours watching him at the front of the room. Trapped behind your desk, you have to clench your hands into fists to stop yourself reaching out to touch him, to pull his glasses off and trace his jawline with your fingertip.

You try and guess which poems are his personal favourites and whenever you're proved right, you take it as confirmation that you see straight through him, to the deep hidden parts that even he hasn't fully uncovered. You try to emulate the easy way that he drops the names of poets into conversation, as if they are old friends, as if they will stand up from their graves, dirt falling off their bodies, and wave. You repeat the names to yourself at night, to help you fall asleep, *Keats, Coleridge, Shelley, Wordsworth, Blake.* Sometimes they sound like curses, sometimes they sound like prayers.

When you meet him in his office, two or three times a week for thirty or forty minutes at a time, you don't talk.

You fantasise about moving to the countryside and buying a farmhouse with him. You want to learn how to make bread, you want to own chickens. You imagine inviting his colleagues round for dinner and impressing them with your own deep knowledge of poetry while you serve them grilled peaches and fresh cream. When they leave, he'll take you to bed and watch you remove your hair pins one by one. Everyone was so impressed by you tonight, he'll tell you, eyes shining in the candlelight, they thought you were so beautiful, so intelligent. He'll be so inspired by living amongst nature, and by you, he'll write his own poems, or maybe a novel, and you'll help him edit it, and when it comes out, he'll dedicate it to you, say he could never have done it alone, that you are in every page.

You have never worked this hard before, and Ella has to constantly remind you to leave your room and eat meals. Up until this point, you have both had similar attitudes towards academia; you go to enough classes to not be penalised for attendance and pull frantic all-nighters in the library when deadline season rolls around. You both read for pleasure constantly and finish your course reading rarely. You used to think that clubs and societies were stupid, a vehicle to meet new people to kiss and get drunk with, but now you love meeting in the library and listening to people talk about poems. One evening, when you cancel on a night out to lie in bed and read, Ella asks you why it matters so much,

I don't get it. You're already with him. Who are you trying to impress?

You can't explain to her that it isn't about impressing him, anymore. It's about trying to understand.

This version of him that you have created in your head becomes so alive to you, that the next time you see him in his office, he looks dull and tired, saying the wrong thing and holding you too tightly. He puts his hands on your hips and you go numb. You want it to feel the way it felt the first time, forbidden and magic, like you were somebody else and he would do anything to have you. You pull away and say,

I read that article you sent me, the one about Wordsworth's depiction of childhood and memory? I've got loads of thoughts.

And he says,

Of course, but actually – could you just email me about it? I have a meeting in twenty minutes.

That night you spend the whole evening at your desk, writing down your thoughts about the article, and when you read the email back to check for typos, you realise that, for the first time, you haven't copied anybody else's writing, that the words are all yours. You lean back in your chair and look at the screen until your eyes blur. *Fuck*, you think, *I get it.* He doesn't reply for days and when he does, it's only to confirm a time to meet.

You get the flu and stay in bed for a week, shivering and sweating while Ella brings you cups of tea. He doesn't get in touch to ask why you aren't in class. You are too sick to read novels, so you fall back into poems, the ones you know by heart. You drift off thinking about nightingales and grassy glades, and dream about him. In these visions, you are connected, intertwined, *apparelled in celestial light.* You are in sweet smelling meadows, beside streams, beneath trees. The colours are vivid, and everything is fluid and changing. When you are awake, your aching body and heavy head long for those fevered landscapes the way Wordsworth did, aching for the stars and the birds, trapped in the hovel of your bedroom where nothing is beautiful, and the bedsheets smell like sickness.

You wake up on the eighth day and the fever has broken, you throw your window open as far as it goes and gulp air into your lungs like water. You feel like a child again, limitless and happy, *the fullness of your bliss, I feel – I feel it all.*

You start looking into applying for a master's in Romanticism, and realise the deadline is in a week. The application states that you need to attach an essay on a relevant topic of your choice and enter the details of who will be providing your reference. You open the email you sent him about Wordsworth, copy the text into a document, and start editing and moving some things around. You are surprised to find that you still like the things you wrote, that your sentences haven't turned into drivel since the last time you checked, which is what usually happens when you reread your own work. You feel proud, you realise, and the unfamiliar feeling spreads around your body and stays there until morning. You wake up smiling and email him to ask if he'll give you a reference.

He becomes slippery and evasive, and whenever you ask to meet, he brushes you off with, of course, soon, and, I'm sorry things are hectic right now. You are afraid to ask him to clarify what he means by 'things'. He stops looking at you in seminars.

One day you walk into class and he isn't there, replaced with a tutor you haven't seen before. You sit down and email him under the table, are you ill? Several hours go by before he replies, no. family stuff. For the first time, you look him up on Facebook. You don't recognise him at first, the picture is a few years old and he isn't wearing his glasses. He's on the beach, smiling into the lens, looking windswept. The caption says, photo cred: and then a woman's name. When you look her up on his friends list you find a beautiful woman. You find a photograph of him kissing her on the cheek. You find a small diamond ring on the fourth finger of her left hand. You find out that she did her undergrad at the same university that he did. You feel like you don't exist, and you have to dig your nails into your palms to check. You draft an email. You delete it. You imagine your future stretching out in front of you like train tracks, the things you are going to do, the people you are going to kiss. You picture him, behind you, getting smaller in the distance. You withdraw your master's application, and your poetry books begin to gather dust on your bedside table. Whenever you think about picking one up, you think about the farmhouse, the peaches, the life you are never going to have. There are two classes left of the semester and you don't go to either. You graduate months later in the dry heat of July and after the ceremony you spot him wandering around the cloisters, sweating in an expensive suit. The sky is completely empty of clouds and when Ella makes you throw your cap in the air for a photo you can't feel a thing.

Kilnacre Cottage

A week after graduation, Ella invites you to come home with her, to her parents' place in the Lake District. She grew up in a small white cottage, with chopped firewood piled in the garden and the backdoor always left unlocked. It's hot, the weather ranging from glorious sun and blue skies to grey muggy heat that chokes you when you go outside. It's going to be just what you need, some fresh air, she says, leaning forward across the train table. You look out of the window as the train speeds past an ugly high school and concrete running track. The air had smelled like yeast from the beer factory when you walked to the train station that morning.

When you were in halls, during late nights or hungover mornings, Ella would tell you stories about her childhood. About Kilnacre Cottage, her family going on walks to the stone circle near the house in the summertime, about picnics and jam sandwiches and washing her hands in the stream. The other girls in your halls flat made fun of the gaps in her frame of reference; she didn't have a TV growing up because her parents preferred to watch old films on the projector; she'd never had a takeaway pizza. Some people would have repackaged their old-fashioned, picturesque upbringing into a cool, hippie childhood, but Ella was too unpretentious to be a poser, and just smiled whenever she was teased. As the two of you grew older though, she realised that you weren't asking her about her childhood to make fun of her, but that the stories made you feel safe, that they helped you calm down when your mind was buzzing. You grew up on a grey, rainy street with dog shit on the pavement and curtains twitching when you went outside. You would have liked to look out of your bedroom window and see sparkling lakes and miles of empty fields instead of streets and streets of houses identical to yours, and your dad swearing at the Renault every morning when it didn't start.

Ella doesn't push you to talk about the tutor, although she listens whenever you need to vent. You wonder aloud why you never looked him up online before and Ella looks at you, sad and pitying and says, I feel like you didn't want to know, right? When she had invited you home with her, she had to ask you three or four times before you said yes. You didn't want to go on a trip because that was something people did after a break-up, and you hadn't broken up with anybody. You didn't get to run away from Glasgow to move on because he never belonged to you. The only thing you were mourning was a relationship that you made up in your head. There wasn't even any chance of bumping into each other, because you knew from checking the woman's Facebook account that the two of them were getting married in Italy, and then interrailing around Europe for their honeymoon. When you told Ella this she said, you're still looking at her Facebook? And you said, no, only sometimes. A few days later, the two of you are on the train, moving further and further away from Glasgow, past tower blocks of flats and big supermarkets and then, as you get further south, pebbled beaches leading to the sea.

*   *   *

Ella's father, Ian, picks you up from the station on his way home from walking the dog, and when he sees his daughter he shouts, Millom taxi service! He hugs her very hard for a few seconds while you linger by your suitcase, your legs sticking together under your flimsy sundress. When he turns to you, he puts his hand out and you shake, awkwardly, feeling like a teenager. It only occurs to you later that he might have been reaching for your bag. It's a ten-minute drive to the cottage, and you scramble to make space for yourself in the back seat amongst the bag of golf clubs, various fishing rods and for some reason, buckets. The dog, a black lab called Frankie, sits in the boot, covered in mud, panting loudly and trying to stick her tongue in your ear. Ella is in the front, moaning about all the shit in the car, and her dad laughs at her and mimes turning up the radio to drown her out. He asks you where you're from, and then proudly tells you that he went to university in Dundee and lived there for a good few years after graduating. Ella looks back at you and mouths, one year, while he tells you both a long story about a stag do in Aberdeen and the resultant hangover, which lasted days. After the resolution of this story, he moves into a monologue about the lack of good bars in Dundee and Ella says,

Dad. She doesn't need your top ten facts about Scotland.

You realise you are holding your breath. You would never speak to your dad like this, but Ian just laughs and keeps going.

When you get to Kilnacre Cottage, you can see Ella's mother from the driveway. She is framed by the kitchen window, washing dishes with an extra tea towel draped over her shoulder. When you enter the hallway, Frankie races past you and skitters into the kitchen, bits of dried mud falling off her belly onto the floor.

I hope you've wiped the dog! Ella's mum calls from the kitchen.

Of course I have! Ian shouts back, winking at you.

You have never seen someone comedy wink in real life before, and you get a compulsion to roll your eyes. You don't know why you get these urges, to spoil things, to be unkind to people when they're nice to you. You shake it off and go through to the kitchen to meet Christine.

She hugs you first, and then Ella, apologising to you both for her soapy hands. You are immediately roped into helping with the dishes. Christine tells you to call her Chris, and hands you the spare tea towel. She points at the rack of dripping plates and says, you dry. Ella is tasked with putting things away, and Chris goes back to the sink to scrub. You start drying the dishes and listen to Ella and Chris catching up. Ella keeps a framed photo of her and her mother on her bedside table. It was taken on her eighteenth birthday, and mother and daughter stand side by side, arms around each other, exactly the same height. They resemble each other closely in the photograph, but seeing them together in real life, you are struck by their near-identical mannerisms, the intonations of their speech. Chris wipes her forehead with the back of her hand, a few minutes later Ella does the same. Ella has a habit of touching the tip of her nose when she's thinking, and you realise that it's something she learned from her mother. You feel sleepy and content in the sunlit kitchen, wiping the plates until they squeak. Christine is gossiping about the neighbour's divorce, Ella is scolding her for being judgemental, but they're laughing the same laugh, falling back into their well-worn roles as mother and daughter. When the dishes are done, Chris debates if it's too early for a glass of wine, decides that it isn't, and sends Ella down to the cellar for a bottle. While she's gone, Chris turns to you, and cups your chin with her hand briefly.

You've been such a good friend to Ella. She absolutely adores you. We are making falafel burgers in your honour.

Ella comes back with a dusty bottle of red wine, and Christine shouts, too hot for red! and sends her straight back down. When Ella returns with the white, the three of you move into the living room to chat. Ian joins you then, and Chris makes a comment about men disappearing whenever there are chores to be done. Ian sticks his middle finger up at her and asks if she wants to set up the projector for a change and Chris looks at you in mock offence, her mouth a perfect 'O' shape. You have the feeling of existing outside of your own body, of watching the scene from above. You can see the tops of Ella, Christine and Ian's heads as they bicker about which film to watch and you feel a wave of love for them, for this family that is welcoming you so readily. When you return to yourself you feel warm and your limbs are heavy and you lean back against the old, squishy sofa, tuck your bare feet under your bum and rest your wine glass on your knee. You start to get warmer then, as the opening credits play, and then unbearably hot, and then freezing cold, and your stomach starts contracting and releasing in that all too familiar way. A stream of nausea and fatigue sweeps over you and you can't stop your hand jerking from the pain, spilling a few drops of wine on the sofa. Ella puts a hand on your leg and whispers, hey are you okay? You shut your eyes tightly and shake your head. You know that you are bleeding, and stay perfectly still, like you can stop the blood spilling out of you if you really try. Ella says, Dad, please can you make us all a cup of tea? and Ian grumbles his way to the kitchen. You hear the kettle click on. Then Ella is brisk, efficient.

Mum, can you go for a minute? She's not well.

You open your eyes a fraction to see Chris looking at you, worried. She nods her head and leaves the room. Then Ella helps you to your feet. You realise that the blood has soaked through your white dress and onto the sofa. Your teeth start chattering and your eyes fill with tears. She asks you what happened to the gynaecology appointment.

I cancelled it.

Why?

I don't know. I'm sorry.

None of that, please.

She puts an arm around your waist and helps you up the stairs, one at a time. She pushes you gently into the bathroom and says, I'll be back in two minutes. You sit on the floor and slump against the bath, breathing deeply. Ella comes back with pads, a pair of faded flowery pyjamas and some painkillers. She says,

I found these in Mum's medicine cabinet. Do you need any help getting out of your dress?

You nod.

Do you want to have a bath?

You nod again. She starts running the tap and helps you pull the dress over your head. You have changed in front of each other countless times, but this is the first time that Ella is seeing you fully naked; hunched over and bloated, with tears and cold sweat soaking your face. It isn't how you pictured it. When the bath is full, she adds shower gel and mixes it around with her hands until the surface of the water is covered in bubbles, and you can smell lavender.

Okay give me your hands and I'll help you get in.

You haven't got enough energy to conjure up a concrete feeling of embarrassment or shame. When you sink into the water, you are warmed from the inside out and you say oh, as you lie back. Ella tells you to shout if you need anything else, and then she's gone, leaving the door open a little, so she'll hear you if you need her. When the painkillers kick in, you feel strong enough to let the plug out and put the pyjamas on. You get into bed in the spare room and Ella has put a hot water bottle under the duvet and an old copy of *Little Women* next to the bed. You text Ella saying, thank you. and she replies, the second we get back to Glasgow I am rescheduling your appointment. As you fall asleep you listen to bodies moving around downstairs and you hear Ella laughing, or maybe Christine, or maybe neither of them, and you're hearing things that aren't there.

Ella knocks on the door to your room in the middle of the night. You're awake and trying to read, even though your head feels tender and sore, and the waves of pain have been replaced with a consistent throbbing ache. You've read the sentence 'I am not afraid of storms, for I am learning how to sail my ship' four or five times, and it has become a jumble of meaningless letters. You keep checking the pad in your underwear and the back of your pyjamas to make sure you haven't bled through onto the sheets. She bursts into the room before you say come in, switching on the big light, and flopping onto your bed, asking if you feel better and telling you that she's drunk a million glasses of wine with her mum and now she feels dizzy. You're sitting on my legs, you say, shoving her over. She sighs and then stands up abruptly, walking over to a small mirror resting on the chest of drawers. She tries to pop a pimple on her chin.

Hey, don't do that, you say gently.

Do you think I am very boring? Ella asks, still focusing on the pimple.

Obviously, I don't think that.

Hmm she replies.

And then,

I am boring. And I am very spotty.

Ella, shut up. I am the dramatic one right now.

She comes back, takes a pillow and puts it on the other end of the bed. Let's top and tail, she says. You try and arrange yourselves so that your feet aren't in each other's faces. Ella says, in a sleepy voice,

This is what it would be like to have a sister.

When you wake up, a few hours later, the pain in your stomach has dulled and Ella's fingers are loosely holding your ankle. It's easy to fall back asleep.

In the morning you feel tired and spaced out from the painkillers. You descend the stairs slowly, trying not to make any noise. You walk into the kitchen and Chris is pottering around. The washing machine emits a low hum, and the window is open. A breeze is ruffling the tea towels hanging by the fridge.

Hello darling, she says, go into the other room and get comfortable, I'll bring you a coffee.

You follow her instructions and go into the living room, which is tidy and smells faintly of bleach. The blood on the sofa has gone, like it was never there in the first place. Chris comes into the room soon after with a tray that holds a cafetière full of coffee, two mugs and a small milk jug. She places the tray precariously between the two of you on the sofa, and points to a rack full of old magazines. You read and drink in companionable silence until Ella comes downstairs, her eyes bleary. Ian comes back from golf an hour or two later and Christine suggests a walk on the beach. You all squeeze into Ian's car and when you get out, the sky is clear and blue, and strands of Ella's hair dance around her face. You imagine the wind stripping the sickness from inside of you and blowing it out to sea. A spray of seawater lands on your face and you lick your lips to taste the salt.

Chris walks in between you and Ella, linking one arm through yours and the other through her daughter's while Ian strides ahead. She asks you questions about your childhood, your favourite class at uni, what you want to do when you grow up. You find yourself telling her that you are worried about the future, that you don't know what you want to do or where you fit. That you found your degree difficult, that you don't think that academia was the right fit for you. You say that you think you were too stupid for uni, really, and you are glad that that time in your life is over.

Christine looks as if she's about to reply, but Ella's voice cuts in, shouting a little to be heard over the wind and the waves.

Literally none of that is true. She loves poetry, she applied for a master's.

You roll your eyes at her, but she doesn't notice, so you clarify.

I withdrew my application. I changed my mind.

Christine bumps her shoulder against yours and says, you're only twenty-one, you need to live first. Find a job that pays the bills, and everything else will come to you.

The anxiety that was building inside of you while you were talking about uni dissolves. You like the way Christine frames things, like you have all the time in the world.

When you get back to the cottage, Chris starts making lunch, and you and Ella sit in the front garden with your books. You look through the window and watch Christine move around the kitchen. Ella leans back to doze. When her breathing slows, you turn your gaze to her. She looks very young, bare-faced, in a T-shirt and denim shorts that are too small for her. She's wearing her mum's flip-flops and her hair is pushed off her face with a bandana. She is so relaxed, always, so confident in her worth and her future. You wonder if you would have grown up like Ella if you had a mother like Christine. You think of what she said to you last night, about being like sisters, and you feel confused. You would like to be part of this family, permanently tangled in their lives, but you don't think of Ella as a sibling. You don't want to top and tail with her or fall asleep on an air mattress beside her bed. You want to lie next to her, your face in her neck, your arm over her body. You haven't let yourself think about what is going to happen to your relationship as you get older. You'd like to think that nothing will change, or that things will change how you would like them to, but you know that you will be pulled away from each other by variables that are out of your control. No matter what happens to the two of you, Ella will always be okay. She will live in the flat her parents own whether you are there or not. If you left, she would find someone else to pay rent to Chris and Ian. There are dozens of photos around the house of Ella in different stages of childhood, with her arms around various other girls. You don't know who any of them are, Ella has never mentioned them. You wonder if one day she will bring someone else to Kilnacre Cottage and they will look at a photograph of the two of you and ask Ella your name.

When Chris calls you in to set the table, you can tell that her and Ian have had a few glasses of wine. Her face is pink, and they keep giggling. Chris wants to talk about her own time at university and tells you a number of funny and sometimes smutty stories about things her and her friends got up to. Ian fills yours and Ella's wine glasses several times. She has recently gotten back in touch with her best friend from university, Janine, who has sent Chris hundreds of photographs from their time as art students. She shows you a picture of herself dressed up as a hippie, eighteen years old in round glasses and flares. She is beautiful, the mirror image of Ella.

How did you guys lose touch? you ask, and Chris shrugs.

We were close for a year or two after uni, but then she got married. She looks a little surprised, and then continues, and then I got married, I suppose. We were busy getting on with our lives.

She puts an arm around Ella's shoulders and says, a little misty eyed, I cannot wait to go to your wedding, darling.

Ella shrugs off Christine's arm and says, oh my god I don't even have a boyfriend, but you can tell that she is touched, and you have to look away for a moment. You still feel delicate from the medication, and you blink hard to stop your eyes from getting wet. Ian fills your glass again, and when you say thank you, he smiles back at you, like he noticed that you were sad. You go to bed soon after dinner, leaving Chris and Ella to look through the rest of the photographs, and Ian to wash up. You are still awake when everyone else comes to bed, and you wait for Ella to come and knock on your door again, but you hear the bathroom light click on, the noise of the flush and the tap, and then Ella makes her way down the landing. There is no knock at the door, and you fall asleep listening.

Leaving the cottage feels like an ending. You can hear what Christine said to you and Ella ringing in your ears as Ian drives the two of you to the train station. You put your bags in the overhead storage and lay your meal deals on the table. You try your hardest to not ask for reassurance, to not seem afraid. You look at your own face in your phone camera and you look pale and unwell. You watch Ella draw her legs up to sit cross-legged on the seat. She's wearing sandals and her nail varnish is chipping off. She's looking out of the window, and you wonder if she's saying a quiet goodbye to her home.

Do you think what happened to your mum and her friend will happen to us?

You ask before you can stop yourself. Hmm? Ella replies, and you repeat the question.

I don't think so, she says, and then laughs when she sees your expression.

No, definitely not.

The two of you search for jobs all the way back to Glasgow. Two weeks afterwards, you get a response to one of your applications, an interview for a customer service job at an investment app. You go into town to buy a blazer. You sit in front of a serious woman and two bored looking men who exchange meaningful eye contact whenever you speak. One week later, they email you a contract and you have to take it to the library to print out. Your signature looks childish against the white paper, stubby spaced-out letters that have smudged together from the drag of your hand. You make two mental notes, 1. Buy a printer. 2. Learn how to write like an adult.

Ella finds a job soon after you, doing communications for a luxury sunglasses company. Neither of you are one hundred per cent sure what this means. The night before you both start, you toast to growing up, to finding the time for creativity on the weekends, to making enough money to go on proper holidays. You FaceTime Chris together, holding your glasses up and shouting Cheers! She congratulates both of you on being adults and blows you virtual kisses. You and Ella get tipsy together that night and download a dating app onto Ella's phone. You swipe left and right and make judgemental comments about people's pictures and bios. She uploads a photograph that you took of her in the garden at Kilnacre Cottage. She is leaning forward and laughing and when she asks for your approval you say, wow, yeah. After thirty minutes or so of swiping, your interest has waned when Ella turns to you and says, okay what about him? She shows you a photograph of a tall, muscular blonde man. His interests are listed as rugby, pints and marine biology. He has no bio. You make a face, but she tells you to shut up and swipes yes. They match and a few minutes later he sends her a message that says hey. His name is Douglas.

Train

You hate your job, but you like the feeling of being employed. You spend all day in an office, replying to angry customers in chat windows, deciding which emoji fits your intended tone. You have a series of verified phrases to use, so you're convinced that everyone you talk to thinks that you're a bot, and you're endlessly surprised at how aggressive people can be when they can't actually hear your voice, see your face. You have been working there for six months and sometimes you feel like you aren't real. When you're on the train home you stare out of the window like you're in a music video and feel sorry for yourself, and make plans to do something worthwhile that evening – maybe try reading poetry again, maybe try writing some – but usually you and Ella just make dinner, or order something, and watch *Gilmore Girls* again. As you're staring out the window and thinking of her, she texts you and says, when you home? And you smile and then you notice a man sitting opposite you, staring.

The train is quiet, past rush hour because you had to stay late, and there is nobody sitting at your table but him. You can't stop yourself from looking back at him and he doesn't look away. His teeth are small and yellow, and you realise that his hand is in his trousers, moving. You look down at your own hands and they're pink because you are so cold. You curl them into fists and press your nails into your palms until they sting. There's ten minutes left of your journey, two stops. The trees outside the window are bare, but soon it will be spring. The man takes his hand out from his tracksuit bottoms and smacks it palm flat on the table. You jump at the noise but keep staring out of the window. You have your headphones in, but no music is playing so you hear him start to drum his hands on the table and say,

Hey, hey.

Then,

Hey, I'm talking to you.

Then,

Why does nobody want to talk anymore?

You take your headphones out and say hi, your voice small. There is a young woman, older than you, but young, sitting facing you a few rows away. She is staring at the floor, her head bent, and you look at her. You can't see her eyes, but your eyes bore into the top of her head, into her skull, willing. She doesn't look up. He asks you where you're going, and you say, home. I know that, he says, where is home? And you don't reply. The train stops, the doors open, nobody gets off, nobody gets on, the doors close, the train starts to move. He starts talking again, did you know, he says, then pauses, smacks the table again. You jump again. Hey. Are you listening? Yes, you say. And he starts again.

Did you know that I used to be a boxer when I was a wee boy?

You shake your head.

I was. I was the best in my group. I should've gone pro.

You say, that's great. He leans forwards, both hands on the table now.

Do you have a boyfriend?

You say no. He starts to reply but the train stops, you get

36

up and move to the doors as quickly as possible, leaving him halfway through a sentence. When you're standing on the platform you watch the train leave. He is leaning back in his seat now, staring at his hands. From a distance he doesn't look dangerous, just sad. The woman is still on the train too, her head still bent forward, and it occurs to you that she might be asleep, but you can't quite tell.

The walk home from the station takes you no time at all and soon you're spilling into your flat, which is warm and full of golden light and Ella's in the kitchen singing, and you can smell onions, but she comes into the hall when she hears you start to cry. What is it, she's asking but you're shaking your head and sniffing and kind of laughing as well and she's holding you up and saying your hands are freezing? Ella puts her hands over yours and starts blowing on the gaps between her fingers to warm them. Douglas comes into the hall and waves at you, then lowers his hand and starts to back into her bedroom when he notices you crying. You try and sit in the moment, try to feel safe with her holding you in the glow of your hallway but you know she's going to follow him back into her room when the evening is over.

Examination Room

On the day of your rescheduled gynaecology appointment, you walk straight past the entrance to the train station and all the way into town. It takes you an hour, and when you lie back to be examined, you look at your trousers and underwear in a little pile on the chair next to you and wish that you weren't sweating. The gynaecologist is quiet and calm, and when she tells you it'll only take a minute, you believe her. She pushes her fingers inside of you and you feel like you are being turned inside out. You clench your fists to stop them from shaking and bite the end of your tongue over and over until you taste blood. She says, is that okay? And you say yes, even though it isn't.

When the exam is over, she says that everything is normal, but that she wants to book you in for an ultrasound, to rule out PCOS. She asks you if you know what endometriosis is, and you shake your head. She gives you a leaflet and starts to explain, but you can't focus, because you are looking at the words on the page, which seem to be written in a different language. She suggests that you get fitted for the coil in the meantime, and you say okay. She looks at you kindly and says, maybe take some time to think about it. Then she leaves the room to let you get dressed, and when you sit up it feels like her fingers are still inside you. She comes back in and says that somebody has cancelled their appointment, and her colleague can fit the coil for you right now if you want and you say, okay, again, like it's the only word you know. She leads you down a corridor into an identical examination room and hands you over to a young man with eyes that are very close together, who tells you to get undressed again. You don't want him to see you like this, naked from the waist down and opened up like a magazine. You cannot speak, so you nod, and he pulls the curtain across while you take off your trousers and underwear. This time there is no warning before a cold metal speculum is inserted into you and you scream. He jumps and looks irritated and says that he can't insert the coil until you relax. You start to cry. He pats your foot and says, some people have a very low pain threshold, but it won't take long, you can cope. After it is over, you try to stand up, but your vision dips and you come to on the floor. The doctor fetches you a tiny bottle of water and sits beside you in silence while you take deep breaths and apologise. He asks if there's somebody who you can call and twenty minutes later, you go outside to meet Ella. You are so happy to see her you have to hold back tears and she says,

I came as soon as I could, Douglas brought the car.

You get in the backseat of the car and Ella sits in the front and turns her head back.

What happened, what did the doctor say?

You look at Douglas's face in the rear-view mirror, and he is focusing on the road. You don't want to talk about the appointment while he is here, you cannot believe that Ella is trying to include him in a moment that is so vulnerable.

It was *fine*.

You can't stop your voice from sounding petulant. Douglas laughs, his eyes still on the road, and says,

Oh dear. Someone's on the rag.

You breathe out hard and fight the urge to say something

you can't take back. Ella laughs and you get hot all over. You look at the backs of their heads in the front of the car and feel like they're your parents taking you home from detention. You clench your fists.

Can you actually let me out here?

Ella turns around, confused, and says what do you mean?

Just let me out of the car. I want to walk back.

Douglas pulls over and you get out and shut the door carefully. You walk into the nearest coffee shop and sit down at an empty table, seething. A waitress comes over straight away and asks if you want something. You're flustered, still trying to calm down, a deep pain resonating through your stomach. You are aware of there being something alien inside of you that wasn't there before. A small T shaped thing that is supposed to fix you. The waitress asks again if you want to order. You say, sorry, I've had a bit of a weird day. She replies,

I'm actually about to finish. Tell me about it over drinks?

Rupert Street

Your girlfriend, Bertie, always smells like coffee beans because she is a barista. She opens bottles of imported beer with her teeth, and she loves The Beatles because her dead dad loved The Beatles. She has reclaimed their song 'Something' as a modern lesbian anthem. She is always reclaiming things. When it comes to Bertie, everything is political, meaningful, just waiting for a chance to be made new again. On your third date, over vegan brownies and peppermint tea, she asked you to be her girlfriend, making it clear that she meant it in an ironic, redefining the label kind of way, not a patriarchal ownership way. You could have cried with happiness, and accepted her offer before she even finished talking, declaring stupidly that you actually love the word girlfriend, and would be honoured to be hers. Six weeks later, you move out of Ella's parents flat, and you move into Bertie's room in Rupert Street. Her flatmate makes jokes about U-Hauling while she helps you carry your desk up the stairs. Bertie laughs so you laugh too, even though you don't know what she means.

Bertie smokes a lot of weed and you get second hand high from it lying down in bed, naked except for a pair of boxers, white sheets resting on your body like snow. She makes you come loudly in the smoky bedroom, over and over again until you beg for her to stop. She asks you if you've ever had sex in the shower, had sex outside, had sex with two people at once. You shake your head no, no, no but you say that you want to, that you'll try anything with her. With Bertie, you are greedy for the first time, you are the kind of person who licks their fingers clean, who is always hungry, who finishes their glass of wine in three gulps, eyes already searching for the waiter. Your body changes, fills out; for the first time in your life, you have hips. Bertie is rail-thin and likes to grab onto your flesh with her fingers, with her teeth. Bertie thinks that social media is a trick of the government to access your personal information, so you delete your accounts, relishing in your newfound unreachability. She sets you feminist theory like homework, so you pretend you like Gertrude Stein and fall in love with Audre Lorde's poetry, even though Bertie thinks that poetry is sentimental. She tells you to quit the investment app and get a job in a bar, so you do. You build a routine for yourself of sleeping late every morning, replacing breakfast with tea and joints. By the time you clock in for your evening shifts, you are pleasantly high, and as a result, find work bearable for the first time in your life. When patrons get aggressive with you, or try and flirt, you smile dreamily, their words grazing you like branches, failing to leave a mark. Your favourite job is cutting the lemons and limes in the back, a task that your other colleagues hate, so you often pass hours of your shift listening to country music and slicing through the fruit, segments piling up on the worktop while your fingers get pruney from the juice. When you get home, Bertie is always awake, no matter the time. The flat is warm and she is making soup, or reading, or rearranging her bookshelves. She is always happy to see you, always ready to stay up talking, always asking if you've started *In Search of Lost Time* yet, and when you shake your head she is condescending, telling you that you have to read it, telling you she cannot keep sharing a bed with somebody who has not read it, telling you that sometimes she forgets that you're still so young.

She comes with you to your ultrasound, and reads while you wait, jiggling in your seat. The appointment letter requested you to come to the hospital with a full bladder, or the ultrasound wouldn't work. You drank three bottles of water on the bus and now you are genuinely worried that you are going to wet yourself. The doctor calls you through, and when you ask Bertie if she'll come with you, she shakes her head and waves her book at you saying, I'll be here.

The cold jelly is smeared on your stomach, exactly like how it is in the films, and you imagine coming back here in the future when you are grown up, when there is life inside of you. You wonder if Bertie ever thinks about having kids, if she would even mind if you couldn't. You ask the doctor what he's looking for and he says, cysts, and then turns back to the screen, ending the discussion. You get your results a week later and you are all clear. You show Bertie and she says, that's great, and you shake your head. This means you need surgery. You sound out the name of the procedure phonetically because you don't understand what the words mean, di-ag-nos-tic lap-ar-os-copy. You schedule the procedure for a date that feels implausibly far away, deep into next year. You ask Bertie if she'll come with you on the day, and she looks at the date and says, sure, if we haven't broken up by then. She sees your face and elbows you in the side, saying, Jesus, I was joking.

*   *   *

Bertie wears the label of her sexuality proudly, on badges, at parties, in casual conversation. She talks about loving women like it's her religion, academic specialty, and life's ambition all at once. When her friends come over, they teach you things about yourself, drip feeding you red wine and sermons on compulsory heterosexuality. Bertie uses you as an example in her monologues, gesturing at you with her wine glass and saying things like: these days, lesbians are so repressed that they're coming out later and later. Or: she didn't even know that she was a lesbian until she met me. Her friends become your friends quickly, but you still feel like an outsider, like you're hanging onto the edges of their inside jokes. They all have such concrete opinions, such security in the labels that fit them just so. You try to strip yourself down to the bones of who you are, think about how you would define yourself if anyone asked. You think *girlfriend* and you look across at Bertie, her pink face in the hot room. It feels right. You look around the room at the group of women talking loudly and laughing and you try out *lesbian*. It fits you okay, but there's a small voice in your head, Ella's voice really, saying are you sure?

Ella reaches out, saying she wants to meet Bertie and asking why you aren't checking Instagram. You arrange for the three of you to have dinner at a Greek restaurant in the West End that you used to go to when you were undergrads. Ella arrives late and looks tired and when you hug her, she smells different, like chemical shampoo and grass. She is wearing a coat that you don't recognise. When you pull away, she tugs your hair lightly and says, oooh haircut! in a high, unnatural voice. Seeing her again makes you feel off-kilter, like time has been falling away without you noticing. It's been almost eight months since you moved in with Bertie and you have only seen Ella twice. It dawns that you forgot to tell her how the ultrasound went, and that she didn't text you to ask. You have been wrapped up in Bertie, and she has been with Douglas, and you wonder if this is the beginning of the end, if you are transitioning out of each other's lives.

The three of you order gin and tonics and a sharing platter and then, as the waiter walks away, Ella puts her hands on the table and says: okay, so what's new with you? You open your mouth to speak, but Bertie says, apart from lesbianism? and laughs. You start to catch Ella up, but you keep tripping over your words, forgetting what she knows and what she doesn't and finally, halfway through a garbled story about work, in which you keep losing your thread, Bertie interrupts and says, oh my god babe, are you okay? You blush and lean back in your chair. Ella says, wait, wait, wait. You quit your job? And Bertie says, yeah, well it was a shitty job, very late-stage capitalism hellscape. You smile and agree but the atmosphere is tense, and the conversation keeps sputtering and dying before it gets off the ground.

Over coffee and baklava, Bertie starts telling Ella about an ongoing drama at her coffee shop. On a work night out, she found out that the male baristas are paid more than the women, which resulted in her confronting her boss the following Monday. You've already heard this particular rant, and actually spent the whole day after the night out going over the facts with Bertie as she paced up and down the hallway. As the story unfolds, you realise that Bertie is leaving out some details and presenting herself as the obvious hero of the piece. You watch her animated face as she talks and talks, and instead of the rush of love you're used to feeling when you look at her, you start to feel embarrassed. Halfway through a sentence you interrupt her and say, yeah but didn't your manager say that the reason they're getting paid more is that they're senior baristas? and she looks at you, confused and hurt.

Bertie leaves straight after the bill, saying that she has to rush to meet a friend for a drink. You were originally supposed to be joining her, but she doesn't mention it, so instead, you and Ella leave together. Without discussing it, you start heading towards the park. You used to walk this loop endlessly when you were in halls, killing time between classes or walking off hangovers. You liked the familiarity, liked seeing pairs of girls with their takeaway coffees and tote bags, doing the exact same thing as you. When you would pass one of these duos, you or Ella would look at the other knowingly and say, hot girl walk, with the other nodding in agreement. Now, you fall into step with her and, although you aren't speaking, the awkwardness of dinner has dissipated now you are outside and moving, retracing the steps of your old life. After a couple of seconds, you nudge her with your elbow and say:
So?
So what?
So, do you like Bertie?
You're trying to sound light, trying to hide how much her approval means to you. Ella doesn't answer for a few seconds and then takes a deep breath.
Yeah of course I do. I mean that was only the first time we met.

Now you're the one not answering, hoping that she'll say something else.

Even though you've been together ages.

You apologise and she says that it's fine, and you both keep walking.

I felt quite awkward actually. I felt like the dinner was awkward.

You feel better now she's said it, now it's out in the open. The two of you enter the park in silence. A man is walking towards the two of you, head down, staring at his phone. You have to break apart to let him walk between you and then, when he passes, you knit back together, closer than before. Ella tries again:

I think I just found it weird to see you like that. And maybe it was extra weird because it's been ages since I've seen you and now, you're all like, new job, new girlfriend, new life. You're very different.

I'm sorry I haven't been great at texting back.

Yeah, I know, it's fine. I also didn't realise you weren't looking at Instagram until like last week, so I've been sending you memes for months.

Memes into the void.

Literally.

You ask how Douglas is, and Ella makes a face and says, let's not talk about it. You walk deeper into the park, quiet again. It's cold and the wind stings your face. Ella says, did you always know that you were gay? Like did you know when we were living together?

I don't know if I am one hundred per cent gay, to be honest.

Does Bertie know that?

You both laugh, but you feel guilty.

She's intense about that kind of stuff. But it's because she knows so much about it. About all the ways lesbians are oppressed by society because of the patriarchy and—

Ella is rolling her eyes.

What? you say, pissed off.

I don't need a gender studies lecture. I've just had one at dinner.

Fuck off.

Ella smiles.

Nah I'm kidding. I agree with her. That's not what I meant. Anyway, I thought you were bisexual.

You don't know what to say. Agreeing with Ella feels like betraying Bertie but disagreeing feels like lying. You realise then why you haven't kept in touch with Ella. It's the way that she always manages to pull things out of you that you want to hide. It's something you haven't missed about her, but part of you is relieved that she's never been the kind of person who shies away from uncomfortable conversations. One evening together and she's already started untangling the mess of contradictions that you've been repressing for months. You come to a stop at the big stone statue of a tiger and her cubs, the one you used to wish on when you were living together. Ella smiles at you: Remember her?

Obviously. Feminist icon.

Remember when I wished for a boyfriend?

Yeah. Your wishes always came true.

You keep walking and eventually you get to the exit by the subway station. Ella sighs and says, Well I have to head home. She hugs you again and you make vague plans to see each other next week, to not leave it so long this time. You retrace your steps back through the park and pause again

48

at the tiger, looking up at her. She's got a fresh kill in her mouth, and her babies are swarming around her, ready to eat. You don't know what to wish for, and even if you did, it feels stupid to play the game when Ella isn't there.

Belgium

You and Bertie go to Belgium for a weekend to stay with one of her friends from her master's degree. You try sour cherry beer, eat hot chips with mayonnaise and race each other up the stairs of the apartment building, getting dizzy as the staircase spirals. The friend doesn't seem to like you much and rolls her eyes when you speak but Bertie says she's like that with everybody. The day before you are due to fly home, you are struck down again by your period, your first in months, and Bertie takes you to the emergency room of a nameless hospital. The air feels cold between you, and she sits silently beside you, chewing her nails and checking her phone. You are curled up in your chair, squeezing your hands into fists as the pain comes over you in waves. You want to press your face into her lap and scream. You doze off and after an unknown length of time, Bertie is shaking you awake, telling you that the doctor is here. You are led through a long fluorescent corridor, identical to all the other long fluorescent corridors that you have been led through before. You sit on an examination bed, rustling the paper and staring at the floor as Bertie and the doctor speak soft French to each other. When she switches back to English, it takes you a few minutes to compute the change and her voice sounds far away as she tells you that you're being given painkillers and getting sent home. In the taxi back to the apartment, you lean against her and feel her arm muscles tense. When you get back to her friend's flat, you're already woozy from the small white pills and collapse straight onto the sofa bed, the room spinning. You are aware of Bertie speaking French again, then tucking you in with a scratchy blanket. You hear the two of them leave. You wake hours later, when they return, and you hear giggling and overexaggerated shushing noises as they lurch into the bedroom and close the door. You fall back asleep and dream vividly. You and Ella are in a church. You are both kneeling at the altar, and she is chanting in a language you don't understand. You are trying to get her attention, but her eyes are closed, and she won't look at you. You start to shake her and scream her name, begging for her to notice you, to talk to you. When you wake up you are covered in sweat and the midday sun is streaming into the living room. Bertie is sitting next to you, frowning. What were you dreaming about? she asks. You don't answer.

When you get back to Scotland, you start getting high more often. It helps with the cramps and also helps you shelve the niggling feeling that something is wrong. Since you saw Ella, you can't get her voice out of your head. She has texted you a few times since, asking to see you, and you keep meaning to reply but you don't. Bertie has been distant since Belgium and these days, when you get back from work, she is already asleep in bed, her back facing you.

A month after the weekend away, Bertie texts you asking to meet after her shift for a drink. You order a bottle of white wine and two glasses, pouring generous measures for you both. When Bertie arrives, she looks at her glass and grimaces as she unwinds her scarf. She tells you that it isn't working, that you're too clingy. It's like you've made me your whole life, she explains, eyes darting around the bar. She tells you that she feels hemmed in, that all of her friends think your relationship is weird. Her tone is completely void of emotion. You don't reply, so she continues. I think it's because I'm the first girl you've been with. I think you've got some things you need to sort before you can be properly out, you know? You uncross your legs under the table and accidentally kick her shin. You say sorry, and then, we've been together a year; I think I'm out. She tells you that she isn't convinced that you're a lesbian, that she thinks you're still attracted to men. You tell her that it sounds like she's been thinking a lot and she asks you to stop being so sarcastic. Your hands start sweating and your vision blurs, but you can't pinpoint any definitive emotion. She tells you that she's going to stay with her friend for a week or two, while you move out of the flat, and then she starts putting her coat back on. She hasn't touched the wine. You look around the bar, helpless, and the patrons that have obviously been listening to your conversation drop their gaze. You take your phone out and look at Ella's contact. Could it be that easy? You know that you should be devastated but you're almost relieved. You call Ella and she picks up on the third ring. She arrives while the wine is still cold and any awkwardness between the two of you has evaporated. When she asks about Bertie you wave your hand and say, we're not talking about it. It's done.

Spain

Soon after you break up with Bertie and move back in with Ella, Douglas and Ella break up too. The end of their relationship is messy and alien to you, and you spend several evenings sitting in bed, trying to read, listening to the two of them fight. You have never heard Ella shout before, but during these arguments, she gets nasty, screaming and swearing. You assume Douglas is the one throwing things, but one night it gets particularly bad, and you hear something smash. You burst into the room to see Ella standing in her underwear in front of her lamp, broken glass spread around her feet. Her chest is rising and falling, and her forehead is shiny from sweat. It feels wrong to see her like this, so you close the door and retreat to your room, where you lie awake all night, wondering how the person you love most in the world could behave like this. You can't get Douglas's face out of your mind, the way he was looking at Ella like he was afraid of her. After a week or so, he stops coming over for good, so you let the image of his frightened face fade from your mind.

Ella loses a lot of weight and when you hold her hand it feels small and fragile. She starts sleeping all day and going for long walks at night, leaving you to sit and watch the clock, worried she won't come home. One night she says to you: I feel like he has stolen my whole personality. You hate Douglas with a passion that almost scares you and you imagine walking to his flat and breaking the windows, making him give her back to you. You have never felt anger like this and when you think about him you feel hot, like your insides are boiling and swirling. You almost enjoy the all-consuming feeling of hating him, because it distracts you from thinking about Bertie, who you haven't spoken to since the night in the bar. It feels dishonest to compare your feelings to hers. You didn't want to talk about your own breakup because your grief paled in comparison to Ella's. Your sadness was small and contained; you were with Bertie and now you are not. Ella is consumed with thoughts of Douglas. One night, when she has been out walking until her hands are numb from cold, she sits opposite you on the sofa and says, shall we go somewhere? And you say, yes.

You book cheap flights to Mallorca, wake up before it's light and buy plastic sunglasses at the airport. Hers: obnoxious red hearts and yours: diamante pink circles. You are both scared of flying and grab each other's hand when the plane shakes, every part of you tense, sure that this time this strange metal creature holding you won't make it off the ground, but it does and as you burst through the cloud cover the sun is setting, orange streaking across the sky like an egg yolk.

When the plane lands, Ella is asleep, and you are thinking about the plans for the holiday. You have been making a list on your phone of the things you want to do and a few local restaurants that serve cheap wine by the bottle. You want to walk through the ruins of the castle, go to the fish market and haggle for lobster, wander through galleries pretending to have opinions about art. The small jolt of impact wakes

Ella up and her eyes shoot open. For a second, she looks surprised, like she doesn't know where she is. She's still wearing her sunglasses pushed back on her head, and mascara is smeared under her eyes. She puts a hand on your knee and says, that gave me a fright, and you smile back at her. It's dark outside, but the air is warm as you wait for the shuttle bus to take you to the airport. The other travellers are spread out on the tarmac, stretching their arms and legs and complaining about how long the bus is taking. When it does arrive, you and Ella are shoved out of the way as a group of drunk men, about your age, push to be the first ones to get on board. When you do make it on, you and Ella are pressed against the glass, looking out at the flashing lights of the terminal, squashed next to each other like sardines in a tin.

An hour later, you are both sitting on the pavement outside the airport, knees up to your chests. Ella is trying to call a taxi in her high school Spanish, and you are drinking a takeaway coffee in small methodical sips, even though it's burning your tongue. In the blur of flights and accommodation, neither of you thought to book an airport transfer, and now you are both tired and irritable. You feel like there is a thin layer of grime covering your whole body, including your teeth, which are furry from the bad coffee and the flight. When you got off the plane and switched your phones back on, Ella had three texts from Douglas, and when she opened them, you caught a glimpse of the first line: I cannot fucking believe that you would—You are worrying that the trip was a mistake.

Next to you, the men from the bus are huddled in a group, with a few stragglers pacing back and forth. One of them is on the phone too, talking in a slow and exaggerated voice, repeating the words, yeah, a taxi, a *taxi* mate. You lean across to Ella, doing your best nature documentary voiceover impression and say, oh and over here we can see a congregation of 'lads on holiday', an incredibly common breed distinguishable by their short shorts and obnoxious mating call. Ella smiles at you, distracted, and then goes back to her phone call. After a few seconds she says ah right, okay, gracias, and hangs up. She shakes her head at you. At the same time, you hear one of the boys clearly say the name of your hotel and then, yeah, a minivan is fine. Yeah great, see you soon. Ella looks at you and you say no, but she's already standing up. She walks over to the boy who was on the phone. He's the tallest one, confident and somehow already a little sunburnt. She smiles up at him and puts a hand on his arm, right over his tribal tattoo. You can immediately tell that she finds him attractive.

Fifteen minutes later you are in the taxi, sitting in between two of the boys. Their solid bodies are pressed against yours, smelling of sweat and booze. They have cracked open some tins for the journey and shared them with you, so you are sitting, balancing the open can on your knee and willing the journey to be over. Ella is in the row in front of you, flirting with the boy who made the phone call, whose name is Fraser. The one on your right, Robbie, is trying half-heartedly to engage you in conversation, but you are more interested in attempting to eavesdrop on Ella and Fraser in the front. You know that she is straight, you've tried not to hold it against her, but you can't help but feel offended that *this* is her sexuality, that she could like somebody like him. The boys are talking about a bar they're going to later, on the coastal strip near your hotel. Robbie tells you that it's free entry for girls if they wear bikini tops and you stare at the back of Ella's head, willing her to turn around and meet your eyes, but she doesn't. She is laughing at everything Fraser says, and the girlish noise is starting to annoy you. It isn't her normal laugh, and you know that she can't actually be finding Fraser funny, because all of his jokes are obvious, childish. It isn't the kind of thing the two of you laugh at, usually.

Later, somehow, you are at the club night on the strip, holding a plastic glass with a pink paper umbrella in it. Ella is dancing on a podium in her bikini top and shorts, already drunk, grinding against Fraser and singing along to the remix blaring through the speakers. You are standing still, the image of the unfun friend, ignoring Robbie's attempts to pull you into the dance circle he and his friends have made. They're all jumping around, spilling beer on the floor, chanting things you can't make out. You walk over to the podium and tap Ella on the calf, putting your fingers to your lips and mouthing, cigarette? She nods and grabs your hand, jumping neatly down from the podium and holding up two fingers to Fraser. When you are outside in the balmy night, away from the loud music, you try and tempt Ella back to you.

Shall we buy a bottle of wine and take it down to the beach? you say, lighting two cigarettes in your mouth and handing one to her. Ella's eyes are glassy and she's swaying a little, her greasy plane hair coming loose from the French plait you did for her. Her teeth have lipstick on them. She looks gorgeous.

No, no I don't want to leave, I'm having fun. Why aren't you having fun babe?

She takes your hand and twirls you round,

This is why we came isn't it? To have fun, to run away from our troubles?

You shrug.

This isn't really fun for me.

She leans against you and kisses your cheek, then laughs and rubs the lipstick off.

Whoops! God I am drunk. Sorry about the lads, I know they aren't our usual type. And sorry if I've been ignoring you a little bit. I'm just trying not to think.

Her face drops and you put your arm around her and say,

I know, *I'm* sorry. Let's have fun.

Ella leans against you, and it is at that moment Robbie and Fraser come outside to join you. They run over and put their arms around you, so you're in a kind of football huddle.

And what are you two girls up to? Robbie asks.

You say,

We aren't girls, actually, we're women.

And then hate yourself for it. Robbie holds his hands up and says, woah. You smile at him and say sorry, and at that moment you make a pledge to be fun for the evening, to let go of your expectations. You can start the real holiday tomorrow, the one you had in mind. Long walks and culture and wine in the afternoon. It could be just like uni again, when you and Ella were everything to each other, when nothing was real until you told her about it. You just have to get through tonight, maybe even do something exciting, for the story.

You go back inside to dance, and you ask Robbie if he wants to take shots. He says, you've changed your tune, and you order tequilas with wedges of lime. He pays. You lick the back of your hand and sprinkle a line of salt on your skin. Robbie leans into you and shouts in your ear,

You know, when you do tequila shots with someone, you're supposed to lick the salt off each other's hands.

You nod and lick the back of his hand, then tip the shot into your mouth. You're surprised to feel an ache in the pit of your stomach when you lick him. He does the same to you and then you put the lime in your mouth, looking at him directly. You think, okay, I can work with this. You lead him into the throng of people and start dancing. You let him put his hands on your waist and it feels good. As you move closer to him and press your back against his chest, for a second you pretend that he is Ella. You turn around, eyes closed, and lean in. You kiss, and his tongue immediately snakes its way into your mouth, hard and insistent. When you pull away, you hear Fraser shout, wahey! over the music.

You get drunk, drunker than you usually let yourself get in a public place, and the four of you dance together in different combinations, holding each other's faces and spinning around, making trips to the bar for more drinks. As it approaches closing time, you and Ella sway back and forth with your arms around each other, shouting the words of the song that's playing. You catch sight of Fraser and Robbie behind you, dancing with each other in the way straight boys do, with their arms across each other's shoulders. You watch Robbie lean over and whisper something in Fraser's ear. Fraser laughs and ruffles the shorter boy's hair. They both look so sweet, sweaty, and uninhibited after all the alcohol, and when you catch Robbie's eye you blow him a kiss.

When the club closes, the boys have lost their friends and the four of you spill out into the night, surrounded by noise and people and the smell of car fumes. You buy cheap bottles of red wine and more cigarettes from a twenty-four-hour supermarket and make your way to the beach to watch the sunrise.

You and Ella are walking close together, arms linked, trying to match each other's steps and wobbling across the sand, shoes in your free hands. She lurches away from you and strips off, running into the sea up to her waist and screaming at the cold. You can see her body silhouetted in the moonlight and you catch your breath at how beautiful she is, the curving line from her waist to her hips. Sometimes when you look at her you feel completely undone, like you would do anything that she wanted. You follow her into the water, shedding your clothes as you go and together you swim out until your toes can barely touch the ground. Robbie and Fraser stay on the beach, and Robbie shouts, be careful girls! after you. Ella wraps her legs around you and leans back into the water, wetting her hair and letting her arms trail above her. The waves are rocking you gently and the core of your body feels hot against hers. You're too drunk. You catch sight of Robbie and Fraser, sitting next to each other on the beach. Robbie is resting his head on Fraser's shoulder, and they are both smiling. You think, this is perfect and then, looking at Ella, I want to touch her so badly.

After your swim, the four of you sit on the beach together, passing the wine back and forth and chain-smoking. The boys have given you their T-shirts to wear to dry off, and they are shivering a little in the pre-dawn cold. They are drunker than you and Ella, and Fraser is trailing his fingers along her shoulders, playing with the string of her bikini top where it peeks out from under his football shirt. He starts to kiss her neck. Robbie leans against your shoulder and you look down at the soft roll of skin at the bottom of his stomach, the freckles on his pale chest. You feel a rush of motherly affection towards him, and you brush your fingers along his soft skin, feeling him tense under your touch. That tickles, he whispers to you, and moves your hand to his shoulder. He is shy now, away from the noise of the club, all his arrogance has gone. He says, can I ask you something? And you nod.

Ella said that you just broke up with someone, called Bertie?

Is that a question?

Was Bertie a girl?

Yeah. She still is one, incidentally.

He laughs. You can tell how nervous he is, and it makes you feel good, to be the one in control. Like you could do anything to him, and he would just have to take it. You scratch your nails along his shoulder, softly, and then harder. He breathes in sharply.

Do you only go out with girls? Or boys too?

I go out with anyone. It's not really a thing.

Cool, cool.

He laughs at himself.

I don't know why I'm being so weird.

You realise that Fraser has stopped kissing Ella when he puts his hand on your knee and says,

Have the two of you ever?

Ella shakes her head.

Never. But I have thought about it.

You look at her,

You've thought about it?

She shrugs. Fraser is grinning at you now and he leans in and kisses you gently on the lips, then leans back quickly, like he's pretending that nothing happened.

Back at yours and Ella's room, the four of you are sitting on the carpet, spinning the empty bottle of wine and taking it in turns to kiss each other. When Robbie spins the bottle, it stops on Fraser and the boys laugh. Robbie goes to spin it again, but Ella says no, no. Play the game. Fraser looks at her, confused, but Robbie leans over the bottle towards Fraser and says, okay, sure. The two boys kiss quickly, and Robbie leans back, then forward again. He puts a hand on Fraser's upper arm and kisses him, harder this time, more like the way he kissed you in the club. You watch the two boys for a few seconds and feel another stirring in your gut. Their two bodies look so big, and Robbie moves across the circle, closer to Fraser. You move the bottle out of the way and look at Robbie's soft arms snaking around Fraser's muscular body. You watch Fraser's jaw clench as he starts to kiss back properly, but then he moves away abruptly, making Robbie lose his balance and fall onto his hands and knees in the middle of the circle. Robbie is blushing and you can see that they're both turned on, Fraser is tugging at his shorts. You all laugh, and then it's quiet. After a second, Fraser clears his throat and says,

Alright girls, it's your turn now.

You and Ella are sitting next to each other, and you turn towards her. The sea has dried on your skin, and you feel sticky, sandy. Her hair is wavy and wild from the salt. You sit up on your haunches and she mirrors you exactly. You move your face close to hers, breathing hard. She puts a hand over your heart, feels it beating and says, are you nervous? You kiss her instead of answering, and she tastes like wine, and you can't believe that this is finally happening. The world shrinks to the size of the two of you, and you kiss her harder, pressing your mouth against hers until your lips bump against her teeth. You put a hand on her hair, and it feels coarse, you tug it a little and Ella breathes out hard. You want to climb inside of her, you can't get close enough. You feel her pull away a little, moving so she is sitting cross-legged, and you kiss her harder and say, can I? against her lips. She nods and you climb into her lap, kissing her cheek, along her jaw, moving to her neck. Your legs are wrapped around hers hips now and your heart feels like it's going to explode. You feel a hand stroke along your shoulders, not Ella's, one of the boys, and you push it away. You have no idea how long it's been when she pulls away and laughs that stupid giggly laugh again, the fake one.

I am so drunk.

You pull away too and notice she's gone red. The boys are silent, staring at the two of you. Fraser clears his throat again and says, so what happens now? Suddenly Ella gets up and runs across to the bathroom, kicking the door half closed. You all sit still as the noise of her throwing up starts to echo round the room. Fraser says, maybe time to call it a night, slapping his hands against his thighs and getting up. Robbie joins him, fiddling with the tie on his shorts and avoiding your eye. You nod and go to the bathroom to help Ella.

When you crouch down beside her and put your hand on her shoulder, she starts to cry noisily, her tears falling into the toilet bowl as she vomits red wine. You gather her hair into a ponytail at the nape of her neck and secure it with an elastic band. You start to rub her shoulders and say, it's okay, in a soothing voice. After she's done, she sits back and smiles tearfully at you, her make-up a mess from the sea and being sick. She rests her forehead against the toilet seat. You can hardly hear her when she whispers, I am so bad.

What? No, you aren't.

I am, I am. Sometimes I think that I am genuinely quite an evil person.

Are you done, do you think?

You gesture at the toilet and Ella nods and leans back, rubbing at her eyes. You get her a glass of water and flush the toilet, and the two of you sit on the bathroom floor together, leaning against the wall, legs out in front of you. She speaks again.

Sometimes I feel so disconnected from the things I do, like I have no power over anything. With Douglas – I behaved so badly. I was cruel. It's nice to be away from that.

You put your head on her shoulder.

I don't think that you're cruel. I don't think you're an evil person.

Ella laughs. Without speaking, you both get up and move back into the bedroom. The empty bottle of wine is still on its side on the floor, where it was spinning. You get into bed and lie next to each other, not quite touching. Your head has started to spin, and you feel sick. Ella reaches out for your hand, and you hold it loosely.

When you wake up, you feel like shit. Hungover but also dirty, like you've cheated on someone or embarrassed yourself publicly. Ella won't stop giggling at everything, being awkward with you. You get espressos, pastries, even more cigarettes, and sit on a bench in the square, dipping your food in the dark liquid. Ella clutches her head and says, oh I feel so sorry for myself, and you laugh at her. You want to talk about last night, but you're worried about making her feel uncomfortable. You don't know how you feel about it, because you aren't used to dissecting your feelings without her. You need to know how she feels, so you can figure out how you feel, it's paradoxical. After a few minutes of silence you say,

Should we talk about last night?

Ella says that she's too embarrassed to talk about it, and then you're both quiet again. After a moment she says,

I'm sorry if I manipulated you into the kissing. I can't really remember everything, but I remember that I enjoyed it.

Your body floods with warmth, and your feelings become clear, even though when you speak again you are stuttering and stupid.

I didn't feel manipulated.

You crumple a napkin up in your hand, and tap your foot against the floor, willing Ella to say something else. She puts her pastry on the paper plate and then touches a hand to your knee and says, stop fidgeting, you're making me nervous. You can't stop yourself from speaking again, from saying the words that you know she wants to hear.

Maybe we shouldn't do it again though, it's too weird.

She looks at you, surprised and then relieved.

I am so glad you said it. I agree, it was just, you know, like kissing your friend. Dumb. Let's not talk about it.

The late morning sun is beating down on you, making your headache worse. You watch a group of pigeons pecking around the square, picking at crumbs. Somewhere nearby, a car starts, a child screams. When you finish your coffee, you dispose of the cups and plates in a public bin and throw the remainders of your pastry on the ground for the birds.

Aberdeen

The day before you leave, the sky is blue, so you walk to the top of the hill in the park with Ella to look out over the city. You can see right across to the West End and the university. The main building seems small from this far away, but it still towers over most of the other structures. A stone carving in front of you tells you that it's five kilometres away by air.

That feels like nothing, Ella says, you could run it in half an hour.

Not on the ground, you reply.

You're acting sulky, you feel like a teenager dragged out for fresh air by your mother. Now you've packed and booked your train ticket, you don't want to go. You turn around and sit on a bench, your back to the view. This way, you can see the hospital, the recreational ground and the beginning of the road you live on. Looking this way feels smaller, safer. You're both silent for a moment. Ella says,

You know, I found a listicle of the top ten reasons why Aberdeen is the best Scottish city.

On you go.

She takes out her phone and starts to read.

Okay, Number one. Aberdeen uni has the oldest established medical school.

She grimaces before continuing,

Number two. It's the prettiest Scottish city. Not sure about that.

She scrolls down, then scrolls some more.

Okay, I've got one. Number five. It's got a beach.

You nod. She's got you there. She skims to the end of the article.

Number ten. The clubs are shit, but in a good way. Jesus. Do you think somebody actually got paid to write this?

She puts her phone back in her pocket and puts her hands on her thighs, standing up.

Right. Let's get a coffee and talk about something else.

You walk down through the park and walk a few laps round the pond, composing different replies to a man that Ella is talking to online. She is being strict with herself, dipping her toe back in after Douglas, and she wants to be sure that whoever she dates next will be kinder, calmer. You can't focus and keep getting distracted by the kids in the playground, the dogs chasing tennis balls, the squirrels running up trees. You have forgotten why you're leaving, so you interrupt Ella halfway through a sentence and say,

Why am I going again?

Because you're finally going to do a fucking master's, she says.

But can't I do that here?

She looks at you, pointedly,

Well no. Because you didn't want to go back to Glasgow uni for your postgrad. No idea why though. Nothing to do with the staff, I'm sure.

You punch her shoulder, and she says, you asked, and you both keep walking. Neither of you mention the other reason. Your relationship had always been easy, but after the kiss in Spain and the subsequent pact to forget it, you don't know how to behave around her. Robbie texted you a few times after you got back, and you suspect that Fraser texted Ella too, but neither of you have mentioned it. Talking about the boys would mean you would have to talk about what happened. You need space, time to re-establish the boundaries that are essential to any platonic friendship. No more sleeping in each other's beds. No more kissing, no more yearning.

When you get back to the flat, Ella helps you finish packing your suitcases, and shoves the rest of your belongings, the things that don't fit, into the hallway cupboard. See, she says, you can always come back if it's shit.

*

You're living in a small, terraced house with one other student who posted an advert on a queer housing page on Facebook. As you get out of your taxi and drag your suitcases up the path, anxiety is making your stomach flip. You're barely breathing as you knock on the door. A boy a little older than you opens the door and you recognise him from his profile picture.
   I'm Finn,
   he says, and then, gesturing at your bags,
   is that all you've got?

*

You are in a taxi. You have been struggling to make friends in your classes, so when a boy from your workshop invited you to pres, you accepted eagerly His name is Drew. When you get to the flat, you text him saying, I'm outside! And after a few minutes, he opens the door. It's weird to see him at night-time, away from the seminar room, and you feel nervous.

Come in, come in!

He beckons, and you follow him into the hallway.

See the thing is,

he says, turning to look at you as he leads you down the corridor,

It isn't actually my flat, it's James's, I'm just staying here tonight after we go out.

You nod, and he opens one of the doors. Inside, a boy who you assume is James is sitting on the floor, a record player in front of him. He's holding a bottle of red wine by the neck, and he smiles at you, then takes a long drink. Around his mouth is faded red, like he's just wiped lipstick off. The National is playing, and the curtains are drawn. It smells damp. You gesture around the room and say, um, I thought other people were coming? Yeah yeah, they are, he says. Well, I thought they were. I'm sure we'll see people when we're out.

You hover in the doorway, holding your bag and coat. You think of Ella, at home in Glasgow, probably watching a film in her pyjamas right now, or maybe out with her man from the app. You imagine telling her about this, about the boy from your seminar who invited you to a party with only one other person. You imagine her raising her eyebrows and saying, threesome invitation or cult ceremony? You could go home and end the story there. Or you could stay. You pull a bottle of wine out of your bag and say, can I stick this in the freezer?

* * *

Later, you're drunk and sitting on the windowsill looking straight up at the full moon. Drew and James are watching you, fighting for your attention. You are completely in control, the most wanted girl at the party, by virtue of being the only girl at the party. When one of the boys makes a joke, the other looks at you for approval before they laugh. You are being disdainful towards them, raising your eyebrows a lot, being both cruel and sexy. You hop off the windowsill and wobble to the bathroom down the hall, where you sit on the toilet, swaying a little bit as you pee. You check your make-up in the mirror, and you have red wine mouth too now, but you don't care. As you're walking back to James's bedroom, the front door opens and a girl walks in. She's fresh-faced, holding a duffel bag, a little sweaty. Oh hi, she says, squeezing past you and going into the kitchen. Your drunken confidence leaves you instantly. For an hour or two you had escaped yourself, been swept up by the wine and the boys. Now you're down to earth, horrified by the idea that this girl has been to the gym and back while you were drinking wine and embarrassing yourself. When you get back to the room, you feel smaller somehow. But then it's taxi time and you're wedged between Drew and James, making accidental eye contact with the driver in the rear-view mirror, feeling a bit sick and very sober.

When you get to the club, it's sweaty and heaving. There are jugs of iced water lined up on the bar and as you survey the people dancing, you see gurning jaws and wild eyes. A remix of a Fleetwood Mac song is playing, and the baseline reverberates through your skull. You have been to nights like this and made a vow with Ella that you would never go again. You hear James say, aw I knew we should have got mandy, and think, what the actual fuck am I doing here. You peel off to go to the bathroom again, and it is full of girls sitting on the sinks and laughing loudly. You open a cubicle door and a girl wearing cargo trousers is doing a line off the closed toilet seat. She holds her baggie out to you, smiling, and you shake your head and close the door. You find an empty cubicle and sit heavily on the toilet, putting your head in your hands and taking a few deep breaths. You are going to leave soon. You start reading the graffiti on the door, tracing the writing with your index finger. You take your lipstick out of your bag and write your name, then Ella's, and then you enclose the two in a heart. Maybe you will stay for one drink and then leave.

Back in the club, you get your drink and start scanning for Drew. You find him close to the DJ decks, holding his phone up with his notes app open, where he's written, PLAY CARLY RAE JEPSON in capital letters. The DJ is shaking his head and pointing to a handwritten sign that says no requests, but Drew keeps shoving his phone against the clear plastic divider anyway. You tap him on the shoulder, and he turns around and grins at you, visibly sweating in his windbreaker. He pockets his phone and grabs your hand, twirling you. You spill some of your drink on the floor and turn away. You feel hands on your waist – Drew's hands? – and they forcefully spin you back around. Not Drew. A short man with a ginger beard and a fade is holding you tight. You put your hands over his and try to peel his fingers off your bare skin, but they won't move. You are a mouse caught in a trap. He leans in towards you quickly and bangs his forehead against yours, knocking skulls. His eyes look like holes. You try to scream but then Drew is between the two of you, pushing the man off you. He says something you can't hear, and the man holds his hands up, backing away. Drew puts his arm around you and says, cigarette, firmly, steering you out the front of the club. You sit together on the pavement, watching people queue to enter the building, and Drew produces a water bottle from his backpack. You are, mortifyingly, hyperventilating, trying to talk and stuttering.

You say,

I was just – It made me feel –

and Drew says,

Okay, slow down. It's okay. Drink the water.

You sit in silence for a minute, Drew rubbing circles on your bare arm. You start breathing normally.

Thank you. That was so – I broke up with my girlfriend recently and I haven't really, I don't know. Thank you for being a good friend.

Drew nods. Then he says,

Your girlfriend?

You nod.

Yeah. I haven't been to a club in a while. I forgot that men can be a bit . . .

Drew smiles,

Grabby?

Yeah.

His arm tightens on your shoulder and suddenly he is leaning close to you, eyes closed, face like a dead fish. You say, Drew, no, I didn't, weakly, and he shushes you, putting a hand on your face. You say, no, again, louder, and he opens his eyes, looking confused. You say,

I want to go home, I think.

He smiles and says,

Aye right yeah. Definitely. Back to yours?

72

And you say no again, like a broken record, like a tease. His eyes go dark and repeats, no, let's go back to yours. You nod, trying not to cry, and he smiles and tells you to wait there. He disappears back into the club to find James and call a taxi, but as soon as he's out of sight, you get up and leave, walking quickly past the queue in the direction of town. He texts you saying, where did u go? but you ignore it and walk the whole way home, shivering without your coat, feeling stupid, like you've made a fuss about nothing.

When you get home, Finn is still awake, hanging up his washing on a complicated homemade pulley contraption and drinking a pint glass full of ice, clear liquid and lemon slices. He asks about your night as he pulls the rope and ties it, his wet clothes swaying a little above your head. It already smells damp, and you know it isn't going to dry by the morning. You start to cry. Finn leads you to the kitchen table, sits down and says, what happened? You are wishing with every fibre of your being that he was Ella, but he isn't, and you can't tell him any of it without telling him all of it. He doesn't know about the man on the train, or the tutor. He doesn't know that you are so tired, just so exhausted of feeling like you have no control over the things that happen to you. You shrug and wipe your face roughly. Finn says, hey it's okay, you can tell me, and you look up at him, and his face is kind, but you can't do it. You can't explain why you're upset because you don't know. With Ella, all you have to do is state the facts, lay out the events of the evening, and she'll know exactly what's wrong. You roll your eyes and wipe your nose and say,

I think I am going to stop dating men.

Finn smiles.

Good for you babe, he says, opening the freezer and pulling out an icy bottle of gin. He makes you a double.

I wish I could make that decision, he says, bringing the glass over to you.

You lay your forehead against it until it goes numb.

That's the freedom of being bi, you know. Just close the hetero side off. Repress.

You smile at him and hold your glass up to cheers. After a moment he says,

I have a good idea.

The birds start singing as he gets the clippers out, and by the time the sun is up, your hair is lying at your feet in a clump like a bird's nest. You stopped measuring your drinks after the first one, and you feel woozy as you look at yourself in the mirror. You and Finn take a picture together in the bathroom light and send it to Ella with the caption: twins! It feels like something has shifted between you and Finn. Maybe it was the intimacy of holding each other still, of seeing his bare neck and feeling the soft fuzz of his hair under your hand. You may not have told him what happened, but he still sensed something in you, the restlessness, the need for reinvention. As you sweep the hair into the bin you giggle and say,

I literally feel lighter.

He laughs too and says,

Next time, we'll bleach it.

As you're lying in bed, drifting in and out of sleep, a hangover already settling in your temples, Ella texts you back. It's almost seven, and she must be getting up for work. Love it!!!! You smile and put your phone on the bedside table, next to the photo of the two of you at a party when you were undergrads, dressed as cowgirls. You sleep past noon and miss your workshop, and when you wake up, you have a text from Drew that says, i don't remember anything! was so hanging in class. where were you? You block his number and think that, actually, you do have control, you can do whatever you want to.

You swap out of your seminar with Drew and fall into bad habits that feel good. Being a student feels different this time, because you're never there and there are no real consequences; the only person you can let down is yourself. Your courses are full of older people; some work full-time and some have kids, all too busy to make friends. There are barely any social opportunities for postgraduates, and the prospect of going to a fresher's event makes you feel a million years old. You and Finn start going out three or four times a week, properly going out, shots of tequila, hunting for afters, chasing the night until it's long gone. Finn is reeling from a break-up and is lonely in Aberdeen, looking for a partner in crime, so he shows you around the gay bars, and gives you the number of his dealer. Your essays and coursework, if you hand in any at all, are long meandering streams of consciousness about poetry, that you often write in one go, when you're drunk or high. You go from being the kind of person who steers clear of risk, to wanting to try everything and everyone, to never knowing when to stop. During this time, you speak to Ella infrequently. You keep making plans to phone each other, but then you go out and miss her calls. When she does manage to get a hold of you, she gets on your nerves. She isn't impressed with your stories, your sexual exploration, your new language of strap-ons and safe words and sex in toilet cubicles. Finn says that she's a prude, that she isn't comfortable with your sexuality, and you agree. When you confront her about this, she is quiet for a long time and then she hangs up. She texts you later that day saying: It is really fucked up for you to imply that I'm not supportive of what you're doing because I'm homophobic. Have you ever thought that maybe I'm worried about you??? You don't reply to the message, and she stops calling.

You and Finn make a pact to try and sleep with someone whose name begins with every letter of the alphabet and you record your successes in a chart on the kitchen whiteboard. You are both stumped by the letter Q. One afternoon, you are sitting at the table, ignoring your deadlines, staring at a bottle of vodka and waiting for the clock to strike 4pm, when Finn bursts into the room, singing, I did it, I did it. He kicks his shoes under the table and flicks the lid off the marker pen dramatically. Under the heading FINN he ticks off the letter Q and writes next to it, in block capitals, QUENTIN. You laugh and say,

Where did you find somebody called Quentin?

And Finn says,

If you split a bag with me, I'll tell you.

You hesitate for three or four seconds, check your bank balance, wish you hadn't, and say,

Fine.

You put on eyeliner and glitter and borrow one of Finn's harnesses, and he debates whether or not he can go out topless in November. When the dealer arrives, Finn goes out to meet him in a silky robe and comes back inside with the little bag of white powder. You cut lines with your library card and sniff deeply, gagging a little from the drip. Everything comes into focus. You dance and start drinking and lose hours in your grimy little kitchen, and then you leave for the club late and run the whole way there to save the taxi money.

When you get inside, you recognise the regulars. You've developed an impressive circle of acquaintances over the past few months, and you find them after midnight, dressed up in costumes, giving you sweaty hugs and asking for free lines and free booze. You go and get drinks and there's a butch behind the bar who you slept with last week. She gives you a free tequila shot, and you lean over the sticky surface and kiss her to say thank you. She puts her hand on the back of your neck and you bite down on her lip. After a long moment, you lean back and she says, wait for me after I get off, and you say, maybe. You search for Finn but can't find him, and when you ask one of your friends where he went, they say he snuck off to the bathroom with a boy. You roll your eyes and dance on your own, free of inhibitions and high on coke and the feeling that you are sexy, fun, mysterious. You think, I wish Ella could understand what this is like. There's nothing behind you, nothing ahead of you, just dancing and sweating and touching people and getting touched. You feel like you are connected to everybody on the dancefloor; blood, bones and something else, something otherworldly. You see a girl dancing in a white dress, and she looks like an angel, and you catch her eye, and you hear her say 'come over here' but she doesn't say it out loud, she says it inside your brain, and you go over and you kiss her and every part of you feels alive and your hearts are beating in perfect time, and you want to say to her let's get married, let's run away together, let's wear the same clothes, eat the same food, share the same body. You try to tell her this, but she looks confused and shouts something back that you can't hear so you just kiss her again and then someone taps you on the shoulder and you spin around and it's Drew.

Your heart is beating too fast and when he looks at you, it stops. You want to leave, or kill him, or hit your head against the wall until it breaks open. Instead, when he tells you he loves your hair, you say thank you, and when he asks you why you switched out of the class, you shrug. Your eyes are darting around, looking for Finn, but you still can't see him and a voice in your head is saying, it is not safe for you here anymore. He asks if he can buy you a drink and you say okay and when he turns away and walks to the bar, you leave. You don't tell anybody where you're going, you just go. You walk home alone and take more bumps from the bag you're supposed to be sharing with Finn. You realise he never told you about Quentin. You get lost and your shoes are hurting your feet and you avoid the eyes of the people smoking outside bars because you know that they hate you and they are laughing at you. Eventually, you stumble onto a familiar street, and you exhale. You want to call Ella so badly, but you know that she's asleep. You open a dating app instead and swipe yes on the first girl you see. She's older than you, tall and powerful looking. You match and message her immediately, she replies, and you call a taxi.

When you get to her flat, it is early morning, but the sky is black. You feel jittery and on edge and you need to touch someone to remind yourself that you exist. She leads you upstairs and you take off your clothes without speaking. She puts an acrylic nail under your nose, and you don't ask what it is you just take it. You come to, later, lying on your back,

78

and there is something inside of you and there are fingers wrapped around your throat. You are aware of other bodies in the room, but you can't move. You hear a faint voice that doesn't sound like your own saying, please, over and over again.

You come to again and it is light outside. You are alone in a filthy bedroom covered with clothes and bottles of alcohol. You get dressed and leave. The air is cold and sharp, and the sun is watery. You don't know where you've left your coat. There is a crack running diagonally across your phone screen and a text from Finn saying, where r u, from a few hours earlier. When you unlock your phone to reply, it dies. You make your way downstairs and out the front door, which is open and swinging back and forth wildly on its hinges. When you get back to the flat, you get straight into bed. You can't stop shivering even when the heating comes on.

Finn starts seeing the boy from the club bathroom and stops going out as much. You pick up his slack. You stop going into uni completely and ignore the concerned emails from your tutors. It is exam season, so most of the crowd that Finn introduced you to are studying at home, and Finn is locked away with Lukas, taking mushrooms and listening to techno and falling in love. You start going out on your own and wake up in the afternoon with bruises you don't remember getting. You go to parties where you are the first to arrive and the last to leave. You throw up every day and can't fall asleep without weed. Your life becomes a routine of coming up and falling down. You stop eating. You buzz your hair every time it starts to grow, but you have to learn how to do it by yourself, because there are no more gin and tonics and bathroom confessions with Finn. Your phone buzzes constantly with pictures of bodies, texts saying come over, messages from your dealer. One night, you are thrown out of a party for stealing a bottle of champagne. You leave without a fuss, taking somebody else's coat and carrying your shoes in your hand.

You get back to the flat and pour yourself a glass of the stolen fizz. You sit on the kitchen table and start flicking through the apps, not ready for the night to end. Lukas comes into the kitchen and gets a fright when he sees you. You apologise and look at him properly for the first time. His hair is long and almost white. He looks ghostly, apart from his eyes, which are dark. He says that Finn is asleep, but he can't drop off, so you make him a drink. You talk about sex and relationships, and he tells you that he is trying to be monogamous with Finn, but it's hard. I just want everything, he tells you, and he looks sad, so you kiss him. Within seconds, you are naked, and he is laying you down on the table and kissing your ribcage, your hip bones, the inside of your thighs. You are closing your eyes, trying your hardest to lose yourself, but the table is uncomfortable, and you can't stop having thoughts. Something smashes and you both jump. Finn is standing in the doorway, a broken plate on the floor. He starts screaming and he sounds like a child. Lukas approaches him, readjusting his shorts and holding his hands out like he is trying to calm a wild animal. Finn looks at you and says, get the fuck out of my house right now. You put your top back on and grab a jacket and run outside and call Ella. She answers on the fourth ring, and you can tell you've woken her up.

I've done something really bad. I've fucked everything.

You drop out of your master's and move back to Glasgow. Finn stays in his room while you pack and when you knock on his door and say goodbye, he doesn't answer. Ella helps you unpack your stuff and after a few hours, it's like you never left. You are quiet and keep jumping at small noises. Ella asks if you want to talk about it and you say no and she sighs and says, we are going to have to have this conversation eventually. You say, do we have to? And she leaves the room. She knocks a few hours later and asks if you want to order pizza and watch *Practical Magic*. You say yes please and while the opening credits are rolling Ella says, eyes fixed on the screen,

No more of this okay. No more hurting yourself.

I promise.

You put your hand on hers, but she moves it away.

Surgical Ward

The night before your surgery, you don't sleep. The surgeon is going to make a hole in your stomach and search around for scar tissue, cysts, things that shouldn't be there. They think they know what's wrong with you, but this is the only way to know for sure. It feels like everything has been leading up to this, the years of pain and gynaecology appointments and knowing that something is broken. You have promised Ella that you won't take anything stronger than over-the-counter painkillers, but as you lie back on the single bed, in the spare room that used to be yours, the call of oblivion is deafening. You think about Finn, and Drew, and the things you did to yourself in Aberdeen. To quiet the noise in your head, you do something that you have been resisting up until this point, you google endometriosis. Your screen is flooded with words: uterus, infertility, pregnancy complications, menopause, woman woman woman. You look at the search results and think, that cannot be me. You don't understand how your body, which is supposed to be a machine that works when you fuel it, could be so foreign to you. You read personal accounts of people with endo on chat forums. You read about suicidal women who can't get their pain taken seriously, teenagers who are going through medical menopause, people in their forties begging their doctors for hysterectomies. You read about the recovery time, some people say it takes a few weeks, some people say it takes months. You read about the likelihood of it coming back, which is high. You read about the possibility of a cure, which is non-existent. In ten hours, your malfunctioning insides will be exposed to your surgeon and his aides, your bare flesh will be opened under hospital lights. You feel so bad that you cannot move, your mind becomes a screen of static. The pain that has been ruining you since you were a teenager feels like it is interlocked with the failures of your personality, the coldness that is only thawed when you are with Ella. You know now that leaving her for the master's was a mistake, that without her, everything in your life starts to unravel. You make two cups of peppermint tea and go to knock on her bedroom door.

She is sitting propped up in bed, watching a film on her laptop, and you put the mugs on her bedside table and get in next to her. She asks if you are okay and you nod, already looking at the screen, feeling comforted by the warmth of her body next to yours. The actors talk onscreen, the volume is turned way down, their dialogue is a pleasant hum. You watch the film in silence for a few minutes and then you whisper,

What if they don't find anything? What if I'm making it up?

You aren't making it up.

If I have it then there's no cure.

She closes the laptop and moves the pillows so you can both lie flat. She faces you.

Whatever happens tomorrow, you will be okay, and I will be there.

She is saying the right thing, like she always does, but you think that you can hear a hint of exasperation in her voice.

You feel sure that she must be getting sick of trying to solve your problems, of being the only person you want near you. You say,

Yeah, you're right, let's get some sleep.

And she closes her eyes. Her breathing slows almost immediately, and you lie there until morning. Whenever you start to drift off, it feels like you are falling, and you have to reach out to reassure yourself that Ella is still lying next to you.

When you wake up after the surgery, you feel sick and your stomach hurts and you can't remember where you are. The last thing you remember is someone sticking a needle in your arm and telling you to count backwards from ten. Ella is sitting next to you, scrolling through her phone. You say, hello, I think I'm going to boke, and your voice sounds strange and high-pitched. You start to giggle, and Ella presses the button for the nurse, who comes immediately and drips something into your IV that makes you go back to sleep.

It feels like you have only blinked, but when you wake up again Ella says it's been a few hours. The nurse brings you a glass of something orange and sweet and asks if you're ready to see the surgeon for a chat. When he arrives, he is distracted, and when he starts to speak, he mumbles and avoids eye contact. You catch the words, endometrial, laparoscopic and reoccurring. You can't understand anything he is saying so you just nod your head and wait for him to leave. When he is finished talking, he stands up and says, so, do you have any questions? And you shake your head. Ella has been looking at you the whole time and says, wait a minute, did you actually get any of that? And you nod again. Ella sighs.

Sorry. Can you repeat that again, slowly? In a way that we can understand.

She takes out her phone and places it on the hospital tray in front of you. She is recording the conversation. He looks exasperated, but he sits back down and starts speaking again. He tells you that they made three small cuts on your stomach, that they found significant amounts of endometrial tissue on your bladder and pelvis and appendix, that they burned it off with a laser, but it might grow back. He tells you that your appendix was so contaminated with tissue that they had to remove it, which accounts for the longer surgery. He takes a breath and then asks you if you have thought about family planning, and for a minute you think that he is asking about your parents. You make a face. He pauses and says, are you thinking of having children?

You say,

So, I have it?

Yes, you have endometriosis.

You are struggling to absorb what he is saying.

But it's gone?

We removed as much of the tissue as we could. We also removed your appendix.

He is looking around the ward, and you feel like you are taking up too much of his time. You are still confused, but it is starting to sink in. You were right, there is something wrong with you. They lasered the tissue off but it will probably grow back, will probably get worse, and you won't be able to have kids. The confirmation of your fears feels almost like relief. You touch your abdomen, the spot where you think your appendix used to be. You don't feel any lighter, but this man has taken things out of your body and disposed of them. You will never know what your insides look like, what your appendix looked like. You lie back on the pillows and go back to sleep.

When you wake again, it is dark outside, and a nurse has come to check your blood pressure. She tells you that they need to check that your bladder is okay and asks if she can help you to the bathroom. When you sit up, your core burns, the incisions feel like they are ripping open. You gasp. It hurts to pee, and you feel like your body is old and used up. While she's helping you back to your bed, you ask her where Ella is, and she says, your friend had to go. When you lie down, you check your phone, and Ella has texted you, let me know when you need to be picked up tomorrow.

The next morning, you are discharged with painkillers and a surgery note that details what happened to you. Your name is written at the top of the paper and underneath, in spidery handwriting, the surgeon has written: *The above named patient attended the day surgery unit for a diagnostic laparoscopy + helium beam to endometriosis + appendectomy.* You wave the piece of paper at Ella and say, they gave me a certificate. Your voice wobbles. She is pushing you to the entrance of the hospital in a wheelchair and you feel high from the drugs that have been pumped into you, your sutures itch and your hair is dirty. Ella hugs you gently and says,

I'm sorry you woke up and I was gone. Let's go home.

The Pond

Will is quiet and serious and doesn't like public displays of affection. Ella meets him at work and within three weeks, he's staying at the flat almost every night, eating your eggs and using all the hot water. You become used to seeing his shoes in your hallway, his 3-in-1 shampoo, body wash and conditioner on the floor of the shower, his hair in the drain. Ella falls in love differently this time, without insecurity or anger. He doesn't shout and she doesn't throw things; they sit at the kitchen table drinking coffee and planning their weekends. Will is a musician, a singer, and he spends his evenings travelling around the country playing weddings and parties with his band. He wants to quit the sunglasses company and be a full-time performer, and Ella forces you to follow him around to various venues in town to watch his gigs. On one of these evenings, you are holding a gin and tonic in a plastic cup, swaying back and forth in the basement of a half-full venue, and you glance over at Ella. She is watching Will play with open adoration, nodding her head in time to the music, mouthing along to the words. You realise that Douglas was just a warm-up, that Ella is standing on the precipice of the real thing, ready to jump.

After they have been together for four months, Ella tells you that she wants to set you up on a date with one of Will's friends. Boy or girl? you ask, and she laughs. His name is

Tom, and he plays violin in the band. She says he is exactly what you need right now.

After you recovered from surgery, Ella got you a job where she and Will work. You are on the bottom rung of the company, packing orders all day in a windowless basement while Ella sits upstairs approving brand strategies and presenting in meetings. Sometimes, when you leave for your lunch break, you catch a glimpse of her in her cubicle, typing or talking on the phone and you wonder what would have happened if you stayed at your grown-up job, if you didn't quit everything the second the novelty wore off.

You have noticed Tom in passing at the gigs, standing in the corner, playing his parts with his eyes closed. You let Ella pass on your number, and he texts you the next day, asking to take you out for dinner. He is visibly nervous when you arrive, fifteen minutes late. You got caught in the rain on the way from the bus stop to the restaurant and you are in a bad mood. He stands up to greet you and goes straight in for a hug, which you accept reluctantly. He is an inch or two shorter than you and seems uncomfortable in his own skin. When he puts his arms around you, your face bumps his shoulder awkwardly. He smells like polo mints. The conversation is stilted, punctuated with silences, and whenever you make a joke, he laughs a second too late, three staccato 'ha's that sound like he's clearing his throat. Your bad mood is solidifying, and you know that your hair has dried badly from the rain. It is still growing out from the buzz cut and you can't stop touching it. You know Ella wants this to work, and part of you feels envious of the comfortable life she has built with Will in such a short time. You remember Ella's mother telling you both about her friend she lost touch with when she got married and you wonder if getting together with Will's friend is the only sure-fire way to keep Ella close to you.

When you get to the end of the meal, Tom pays and leads you out of the restaurant, his hand on your back. You let him walk you to the bus stop and kiss you on the cheek. On the way home, you text Ella saying, no luck with tom, and she replies with three crying faces. When you get into bed a few hours later, your screen lights up with a message from Tom that says, I would love to see you again.

Whenever he takes you out, he insists on paying. You fall into a routine of seeing each other two or three times a week; cinema trips, laps around the park, dinners and drinks. He loves the park unselfconsciously; tells you facts about its history and quizzes you on the types of trees you pass on your walks. Ah ah, he shouts, delighted, mimicking the noise of a game show buzzer. That's an oak tree, not an elm. Better luck next time. You hate how charming you find him when he's being nerdy. If Ella told you that Will loved tree spotting, you would never let her forget it.

You build inside jokes and traditions. He teases you for reading fiction and you tease him for reading non-fiction. After a month, you start sleeping together. The first time is awkward, his hands are shaking, and you can't stop talking, but it gets better. You have made a quiet pact to yourself to never have sex with him when you are drunk, to never have sex with him as a way of escaping yourself. This is easier than you thought it would be, because when you are with him, you feel quiet inside. You never feel like you are supposed to be somewhere else. He doesn't mind that you don't sleep well, and sometimes, you go into the living room together late at night and watch films until the sun comes up. Tom likes films with guns and violence, the kind where girls show up in low cut tops and then get murdered and avenged. You like long films with little to no plot, about women finding their way in the world. When you have a particularly bad night, he puts on one of your favourites without question. This unspoken submission to you makes you feel safe.

You wonder if this is love. Choosing films and holding hands and deciding what to have for dinner. Sometimes you think it is. Sometimes you think it's just the warm feeling of knowing somebody. He starts buying peaches for you in his food shops, you start keeping Heinekens in your fridge. Sometimes he sends you links to articles saying, you'll like this, and usually he's right. But he doesn't make you laugh, and every now and again, when he puts his arm around your waist, you have the urge to move it away. You can't fight the feeling that there is something wrong with you, that you are made badly, that you are cold in some rigid, unchangeable way. When you confess these fears to Ella, she tells you that being sick doesn't make you unlovable.

You and Tom have confided in each other about your past relationships. He has had one serious girlfriend; a girl he met in school and stayed with through university. When he talks about her, he can't make eye contact with you, and you can tell that he is trying to compress his emotions. When she broke up with him, he didn't go on another date for three years. Since then, he has had a string of failed almost connections; and has been ghosted often. He doesn't seem to have any close friends, but when you tell Ella this, she says that men in their late twenties don't have friends, as a rule. You point out that Will has friends, and Ella tells you that he is the exception. In exchange for Tom's confession, you tell him about Bertie and the tutor. You even tell him about Aberdeen, and you are surprised that it doesn't hurt you to talk about any of it because it feels like it all happened to somebody else. Tom is uncomfortable with your past promiscuity, with your unwillingness to pick a gender and stick to it. He asks you if you're bisexual and you shrug and say that you haven't really thought about it. Tom replies that he has never done anything in his life without really thinking about it. You move over this awkward patch by reassuring Tom that you're ready to settle down, that you've made mistakes but now you have matured into a different person. He thinks you should grow your hair out long again, like pictures he's seen of you from your undergrad. You look so pretty like that, he says, holding your face gently.

On your six-month anniversary, Tom tells you that he loves you, and as soon as you hear the words, your blood runs cold. You can't hide the shock on your face, and he tells you that it's okay, you don't have to say anything back, you can take it slow, he just wanted to tell you. From that moment, you know that you can't do it, that you have been deceiving yourself by playing house with him. Your cosy routine starts to feel like a prison schedule, you get angry when he is kind to you, you retreat further into yourself while he tries his best to draw you out. You make no effort to hide your irritation and then you get angry when he doesn't bring up your bad behaviour. You know he has picked up on something because he has started acting like you are about to explode; hanging off your arm and texting you constantly when you aren't with him. This makes you even angrier, that he has so little self-respect that he would allow himself to be treated so badly. You find his weird, disjointed laugh unbearable. You notice that he smacks his lips together after he takes a sip of beer, and always zips his jacket up right to the top. You keep trying to start arguments with him, but he won't bite, and whenever you raise your voice, he looks like a dog that's afraid of being kicked.

Ella decides that she wants the two of you to go and watch Will and Tom perform, you haven't been spending much time together and she misses you. You get ready together like you did in uni and revert back to your younger selves, gossiping and doing each other's eyeliner and gulping your wine. The two of you wait for the taxi, sharing a cigarette, and you ask Ella why she's shivering. She tells you that she's shivering because it's freezing, but you feel like you're on fire. You stumble as you get into the car and think, *oh*, drunk.

When you get to the venue, Will and Tom are waiting outside. The tip of Tom's nose is pink and feels icy when he kisses your cheek. Why is everyone so fucking cold! you say, too loudly, and go inside without waiting for the others. You order four bottles of beer at the bar, and four tequila shots, which Will, Ella and Tom take reluctantly. You see Ella make a face at Will out of the corner of your eye. You try and make her dance with you while the boys play, but she isn't into it, and you spin her around so roughly she almost falls over. She motions to you that she wants to go for a cigarette and when you get outside, she says, what is up with you? You tell her that Tom told you he loved you, and she looks confused.

I don't understand what the problem is?

Okay? you reply, sulky like a teenager.

Did you say it back?

No.

Are you going to?

No.

Ella makes a face again, the same one she made to Will in the bar. Then she says, okay. Yikes. And you feel so angry you want to stamp your foot on the floor and say, it's not fair. Ella pokes you in the arm and says,

Do you want to talk about it?

Obviously not.

And you both smile at the awkwardness of the situation, and the anger whooshes out of you all in one go. Ella says, no double wedding then, and you both burst out laughing. You know that you have to end things, but you don't have to do it right now, so the laughter is mixed with relief. Ella takes a sip of her drink and smacks her lips together loudly.

Right, shall we go in then?

And you laugh even harder and say, oh my god I can't believe you noticed that. You go back inside, and Ella gets you a water to sober you up. You leave as soon as the gig is over, telling Tom you have a headache and letting Ella go back with Will. You get into bed and turn off your phone. You stare at the ceiling and decide to do it tomorrow.

You text Tom to meet you in the park, and when you see him waiting by the playground, you clench your fists and think, twenty minutes and it's over. He says hello and kisses you on the cheek, and then the two of you start walking the loop of the park that you always do, hands in pockets. It starts to rain. He is trying to talk to you, but you can't focus. He tells you he's thinking about growing a moustache and you say, Tom I have something I want to tell you. You gesture at a bench a few metres in front of you and he says, no let's sit by the pond. You walk a little further and sit on his favourite bench, the one with a memorial plaque that reads, *for Joanna, who loved to sit here.* He thinks it's romantic. You sit at one end of the bench, and he at the other. He traces the raised lettering on the plaque, smiling to himself. You say, I think something is missing for me, and he turns to face you quickly and says,

What?

Sorry.

What's missing? He looks confused.

You look down at your left hand and tap each one of your fingertips against the pad of your thumb before you answer.

I can't articulate myself properly. I'm just not there yet.

His voice is very quiet and low-pitched when he answers.

What do you mean, yet? Do you think you'll get there soon?

You shake your head.

Do you think you'll get there, ever?

I don't know. I mean, no, probably.

He looks away from you, back to the pond, and you follow his gaze. You watch a duck move cleanly through the water to the nest. He replies,

Is it because you're a lesbian?

You laugh at the absurdity of the question, and then immediately regret it when he looks at you and you can see tears in his eyes. His voice is shaking.

Please don't make fun of me.

No, that isn't what's happening. It has nothing to do with that, I just feel like . . .

You don't know what to say. The two of you sit in silence and then Tom stands up and puts his jacket on. You start to get up as well and he says,

No, don't get up. I want to leave.

He starts to walk away and then he turns back,

You know what?

He takes a deep breath and then says slowly, enunciating each word clearly,

You have led me on.

He walks away and you watch him, willing yourself to feel sad or angry or any feeling that isn't a hard surety that you have done the right thing. You text Ella when you walk home, to see if she's in the flat and she texts back saying, no with will. You go to the shop to pick up milk, bread and yoghurt, let yourself into the flat and put your shoes on the shoe rack. Then you make lunch, tidy up, water the plants, and apply for a few jobs. Impulsively, you google Bertie's full name. You haven't looked her up since the break-up, almost two years ago now and you're surprised to see that she has a few social media accounts, meaning she must have changed her opinion on internet surveillance and the dangers of having an online footprint. Apart from that, she is the same, same friends, same haircut, same political rants, and judgemental wording. You think about following her but decide not to. Later, when you're about to go to bed, Tom texts you.

Hi. I think you might be confused about how you're feeling, and that's okay. I can move fast in relationships, I've been told that before, but I don't think that's what this is. It's been six months. It's been great between us. I've been letting you set the pace but

95

now I think I should take the reins a bit. You've never had a serious relationship before and that isn't your fault. I do love you, and I think we have more to talk about. Tom.

You type out a few different responses in your notes app but everything you write feels cold and robotic. You send Ella a screenshot of the text with the message,

Am I insane or is this a really bizarre message to send somebody after they've just broken up with you?????

Ella replies immediately, coming home now

When she gets back, she helps you write a message to Tom. She disregards your earlier drafts, and in the end, you just send what she has written for you.

I'm really sorry. I loved spending time with you, but I don't think we should see each other again.

The message shows up as delivered immediately, and a few seconds later, the ticks turn blue, so you know that he's read it. He doesn't reply, and when you check his social media, you've been blocked on everything. You show Ella the blank space where his account used to be and she says, so I guess you won't be coming to the gigs anymore. You laugh, but over the next few days you can't shake the feeling that you are reacting in the wrong way. You don't miss him or regret your decision, but the next time you can't sleep and turn the light on to watch something, your mouse hovers over one of Tom's favourites and you remember the way he sat next to you for hours, watching films in complete silence, forcing his eyes to stay open so you wouldn't be alone.

Bellahouston

Visiting Rowan on the train feels special, almost sacred. The twenty-minute journey out of the city centre and into the suburbs becomes time that you dedicate only to thinking about him and preparing yourself to be in his company. You fall into a routine of applying make-up and doing your hair. He likes your dark eyebrows, so you make them darker with brow gel. He likes old film stars, so you paint your lips red and sweep your hair off your face. The ritual of making yourself beautiful for someone else is brand new to you, and it feels excitingly feminine. Laying out the brushes on the train table reminds you of when Ella used to read your tarot in uni, the slow, deliberate way she would turn over the cards and tell you what was going to happen to you.

The new make-up routine doesn't match your clothes, and you find yourself wandering around shops that you and Ella would never usually go to; the kind with retro silhouettes, cinched waists, plunging backs. The first time you buy one of these dresses and show Ella, she doesn't try to hide her surprise. You both still dress like students and over the years your clothes had travelled back and forth between each other's rooms until you ended up with a kind of communal wardrobe of wide leg trousers, sack dresses and oversized denim jackets. Ella once joked that if it didn't smell like your grandpa's house and come from a Cancer Research shop, you weren't interested. Strangely, you didn't care that she hated it, because you had already sent Rowan a photo of the dress when you tried it on in the changing rooms, and he said you looked like Marilyn Monroe. When you hung it up on the clothes rail in Ella's room, because there wasn't space in your wardrobe, she said, oh yeah, that'll be great for my rockabilly club night, and you told her to fuck off, smiling, her words sliding off you like rain.

The first time you make the journey, Rowan meets you on the platform, so you don't get lost on the walk to his house. You see him before he sees you. He is waiting in the wrong place; you are in the front carriage, and he is halfway down the platform, so you get to glimpse him standing still while you are in motion. You get off the train and start walking towards him. He does the same, and you share an awkward smile as you close the distance between the two of you. When you meet, you wonder if you're going to hug or shake hands, but he kisses you. His lips on yours, his hands on your face, and you feel the gold ring on his middle finger press into your cheek. The kiss lasts a long time, and when you pull away and look at him, you think, simply, I'm happy.

As you walk back to his, you pass streets and streets of beautiful houses. It is a decidedly grown-up area, and you feel envious of the people who live here. You cannot comprehend how different their lives must be from yours. You look at Rowan walking next to you and he looks perfect. When you first saw him, watched him struggling with his bags and marking, he looked awkward and gangly, ducking to get through the doors and folding his legs to fit in the seat. Here, he carries himself easily, almost elegantly. He catches you watching him and says, yes? And you shake your head, smiling. You point to a house at the end of the street and say, wow, that house literally has a turret. He laughs and says, that's where I live, reaching for your hand. As you walk towards his house, you pretend that he is your husband, that you have been together for years. You imagine this life so vividly that you can almost feel the weight of house keys in your empty pocket.

You met on a train. You had been to stay with Ella and her parents at the cottage and caught the train back alone so you didn't miss work. You watched him get on, heaving an expensive-looking suitcase monogrammed with the initials R.M. His glasses were covered with smudges, sliding down his nose, and in addition to his luggage, there was a collection of papers scrunched into one hand. You were reminded of the tutor you slept with in uni, almost four years ago now. This man was older, but the two of them shared the kind of dishevelled, posh boy look that you have always found depressingly sexy. He sat down opposite you, a little out of breath, and said,

I feel like I spend my life running for the train.

You smiled at him and watched as he tried to straighten out the creases in the sheets of paper. What are those? you said, pointing. He grimaced,

I'm marking an essay; I like to print them out so I can annotate by hand.

You had to resist the urge to roll your eyes, not at him, but at yourself, at the predictability of your attraction. Are you a high school teacher? you asked, already knowing the answer. He told you no, he's a philosophy professor, and you continued talking for the next three hours, until the train pulled into Glasgow Central.

You stood in the middle of the station, facing each other, Rowan's suitcase between you as people rushed past for their trains. You were waiting for him to ask for your number, starting to worry that you'd misjudged the situation completely. But then he said,

did you know that there's a champagne bar in the station? I've never been.

Fifteen minutes later you were clinking your glasses together and Rowan was toasting to the outlandishness of drinking champagne with a stranger in a train station. You added, at 3pm on a Wednesday, and drained half of your glass, already giddy. You couldn't help but clock the price of the bottle when Rowan ordered. The thought that you would have to work an eight-hour shift to afford the cheapest bottle on the menu drifted into your head, but you pushed it out. Rowan asked what you do, and you watched his nose crinkle almost imperceptibly when you told him that you worked in a basement, packing sunglasses. You rushed to add that it was just a day job, that you always wanted to go into academia, but you've had some setbacks. He smiled when you mentioned starting a master's; a genuine smile without condescension, and said, I would love to hear about your research. You make it seem like you dropped out of your postgrad due to funding issues, that you're saving up to go back, and he listens. The two of you made your way through the bottle while he asked you questions about literary tastes and area of study. You could feel yourself getting flushed from the champagne and also the power of his undivided attention. It made you realise how rare it is for someone to look you in the eye. He reached for your hand across the table and his skin felt cool against your sweating palm.

Can I get your number? I want to read your work,

he said, and you nodded, wanting so badly to be the kind of person that had work for him to read. You let him signal to the waiter to bring more champagne.

When you got home, you called Ella and told her everything. You spoke uninterrupted for almost ten minutes, and when you finished, she sighed dramatically and said, Jesus Christ. You could tell that she was impressed, despite herself. Are you going to see him again, do you reckon? she asked and you said, yeah, he's cooking me dinner tomorrow after work, I'm getting the train.

When you get to his house, you barely register the hallway before Rowan kisses you again. You make your way upstairs like you're in a romance novel, shedding clothes on every step and falling onto the bed in your underwear. The sex is good, passionate and romantic, a lot of face stroking and whispered compliments. But afterwards, when you're lying next to each other and Rowan lights two cigarettes in his mouth and hands you one, it feels like he is performing for you. The two of you had gone out for a cigarette at the champagne bar, and Rowan had coughed when he inhaled, admitting that he had never been much of a smoker. You imagine him going out to buy the cigarettes before you came over, maybe even smoking a few for practice. It makes you feel oddly touched that he would consciously adjust his behaviour to match yours in this way. It makes you wonder if he is more aware of the age difference than you thought, if he is trying to appear younger or more laid back to please you. This thought makes you feel incredibly tender towards him, and you lean over and kiss him on the cheek. He tells you to stay in bed, and goes downstairs for twenty minutes or so, returning with bowls of steaming udon noodles with green vegetables and sesame oil. You slurp the noodles side by side in bed, and you ask him greedy questions about his life; you want to know everything he has ever done, every thought he has ever had. The food is delicious, and you are high on the sex and his handsome face, and the fact that you are in bed with somebody who has bok choy in their fridge. He tells you that he was married before, and still talks to his ex-wife regularly. When he tells you her name is Jane, you realise that she is a senior lecturer at your old university, although your paths never crossed. She worked in the English Literature department and sometimes the tutor would make comments about how difficult she was. You ask him to tell you more about their relationship, and e says that she could be high maintenance. You tell him that when you were at uni, she had a reputation for being harsh, and he laughs, and tells you that sounds about right.

You slip into his life like you have always been there. You stay at his house three or four nights a week, and he cooks dinner, standing up at his breakfast bar and chopping vegetables while you sit on a stool opposite him, chin in your hands, under his spell. When you are lying next to each other, after you've had sex, eyes heavy, he tells you about the things that he wants. He wants children, Jane didn't, he wants to be a senior lecturer, he wants to publish a book of essays. When he turns his gaze on you and asks what you want to achieve, you are stuck. You have always tried not to think too far forward. He helps you map a future in which Ella is not the main character. On these nights, when he talks, you believe him. He makes it clear that he wants a future with you, when he talks about getting married again and having kids, you are in the starring role. You wish that you could capture this period of your life in a vacuum, continue to live in a bubble that is just you and Rowan. You understand what Christine was talking about years ago, how friends can fall in love and move out of each other's lives. You feel nothing but tenderness towards Ella now, the panic of losing her has dislodged itself from the bottom of your stomach and dissolved into your bloodstream. You text back and forth, send each other selfies and hang out whenever when the two of you are in the flat together. Being with her becomes easy and uncomplicated, like it was when you were in uni. You get to know Will better, and begin to appreciate his steadiness, his dependability. You feel happy that you and Ella are developing such a healthy relationship, and you can tell that she is relieved that you are finally sorting yourself out.

One afternoon, you and Ella are catastrophically hungover and you are supposed to meet Rowan for lunch. You text him to cancel, explaining your predicament, and he asks if he can drop you off some supplies. When he arrives, you and Ella are lying on the sofa in your pyjamas underneath a duvet you've dragged through from your bedroom, watching *Love Island* and laughing at things that aren't funny. When Rowan arrives, he has just come from lecturing and you look at him in the doorway, holding a white plastic bag and his leather wallet, still wearing his shoes. He looks out of place in your flat, which is messy and smells vaguely of weed and damp clothes. His ironed white shirt makes the walls look grey. He introduces himself to Ella too formally, and she giggles and apologises for not getting up. He doles out Lucozades and packets of crisps, like a dad at sports day.

Last night was so messy I actually feel like I'm going to die.

Ella clutches her head and Rowan laughs awkwardly. You feel ashamed of her for the first time in your life, ashamed of the life you are living, worlds apart from Rowan's beautiful house on his street full of trees. You end up going home with him that afternoon, and going straight to bed, kissing and lying back on his clean sheets, as the sunlight streams into the room. He takes you out for dinner that night, and you wear a pretty dress and soothe your hangover by getting back on it, ordering a bottle of red wine without checking the price. You relish the contrast of your evening compared to last night with Ella, where you drank spirit mixers and got chips on the way home. Rowan gets tipsy off two glasses of wine, and you make his cheeks turn pink when you lean across the table to kiss him. You ask him what he thought of Ella, and he trips over his words.

She's very nice. She's different from you . . . maybe a little immature?

Nobody has ever thought that you were the mature one before, and you wonder if you behave differently with Rowan without knowing it. From that moment, you view yourself as living two separate lives; the twenty-five-year-old who still works a crap job and curses the council tax bill every month, and Rowan's girlfriend, who has opinions on politics and what kind of wine goes best with seafood. You like being a chameleon, putting on your vintage dresses and applying your make-up, becoming someone else. While you're walking home, Ella texts you saying, loved your sexy professor btw.

You show Rowan, and you can tell that he is pleased. You realise that he feels like a chameleon with you too. He gets to be the older boyfriend with a good job, who pays for things and impresses your friends. When he talks about Jane sometimes, you can tell that he feels emasculated by her academic reputation and the fact that she didn't need him. When the two of you first talked about your childhoods, you told him you don't speak to your parents at all. It felt more simple than the truth, and you could see him storing this information away, adding it to the lie you told him about dropping out of the master's. You realise that all relationships are transactional, that people fall in love because of the way their partner makes them feel, the person they allow them to pretend to be. He pays for your dinners and helps you with bills, and you let him think you're alone in the world, a bright mind held back by financial circumstances. It works for you both. You need him and he wants to be needed. It makes you wonder about Ella, what you are to each other. She has always been the most important relationship in your life, your moral compass and safe place. But you don't know what you give to her, whether you are a positive figure in her life or something that she wishes she could let go of.

Dinner Party

You agonise about what to wear, how to behave. You get ready at the flat and Ella sits on the floor in your bedroom, rejecting every outfit you try on. She is getting on your nerves.

Do you have something sort of chic and sexy but also grown-up?

You throw a pair of trousers at her. In the end you wear all black and put your hair up. Ella thinks you should wear a lot of make-up and you don't think you should wear any, so you compromise by wearing a normal amount. You get a taxi to the address that Rowan sent you and he meets you outside. You are late, so he's already been inside and had a drink, and he kisses you three times, once on each cheek and then on your forehead. You link arms with him and go inside. A woman holding a baby introduces herself as Jen, the hostess, and asks if you want red or white wine. While she fetches you a glass, she hands the baby to you, and says, hold Agnes for a sec. You take her, and she looks up at you, blinks, then starts to cry. You bob up and down, a little frantically, and make soothing noises. Another woman approaches you and holds her arms out for Agnes. Her name is Diane. Jen and Diane's husbands introduce themselves as Keir and Jonathon, but you don't know whose husband belongs to whom. They both have red faces and are sweating in their dinner jackets. Rowan has disappeared, so you follow Jen into the kitchen and ask if there's anything you can do to help with dinner. She says, no, no, and gives you a glass of red wine, even though you asked for white. You say, thank you, and then there is an excruciating pause. You ask how old Agnes is, and Jen starts to tell you about how exhausted she is, how she hasn't had a full night sleep for six months, how Jonathon doesn't wake up when she cries. She laughs as she talks, but her tone is bitter. You think, okay Jonathon is her husband, and try to join in with her bitching without actually saying anything negative. Diane comes back in and says,

We have been dying to meet you. Rowan told us you met on a train, it's so romantic.

You nod and start to say something, but Diane turns to Jen and says,

Please do *not* let Keir drink as much as last time. We told the babysitter we'd be back by eleven.

You look at the clock on the wall, it is seven o'clock. You think, four hours and I can leave. Jen continues her evisceration of Jonathon in hushed tones, and you go back into the living room to find Rowan. The three men are standing in the corner, open bottles of beer in their hands, talking about the bin schedule. You think you have misheard, but no, they are genuinely talking about bins.

Number thirty-five always put their recycling in our blue bins and it's getting past a piss-take now. Di thinks I should go over and have a word with them.

You stand next to Rowan and he immediately puts his arm around you, drawing you close to him. Jonathon gestures at you with his beer bottle and says,

You probably think we're a bunch of old farts, talking about this stuff.

You smile and say, oh no, a second too late and the three

men laugh. Keir asks what you do, and you start to tell him about work, but Rowan interrupts and says, she's a writer. You smile, and they ask you a few questions about what you're working on, but your answers are non-committal, and the conversation dies. You excuse yourself to go to the bathroom and Ella has texted you.

how is everything going????

remember our Mexican dinner party in second year? exact same.

lol. who puked in the kitchen sink this time?

if i keep having to listen to chat about bins . . . it's going to be me.

The women serve dinner, a type of fish you've never had before in an oily sauce, with big bowls of salad, bread and potatoes in the middle of the table. Agnes is sitting in a highchair with Jen on one side and you on the other. Jen alternates between feeding the baby and scooping food into her own mouth, trying to hold a conversation with Diane at the same time. At one point, she accidentally holds Agnes's plastic spoon heaped with mashed potato up to her own mouth and when she notices her mistake, she laughs and rolls her eyes. Rowan is on the other side of the table, talking to the men. You tune in and out of both conversations, eat your food and say very little. After fifteen minutes or so, Jen and Diane both look at you, and you realise that somebody has asked you a question,

Sorry, I totally zoned out. What did you say?

Diane was just asking if you've ever thought about having

children?

Her tone is exactly the same as your surgeons, and you have to stop yourself from laughing. You realise Rowan is looking at you as well, waiting for your answer.

I think so, but not for a while.

Rowan doesn't know you are sick, and apart from the occasional mood swing, the coil has been working. You aren't the kind of couple that talk about periods or bodily functions, and you appreciate the privacy because it means that you have never had to navigate a conversation about your potential fertility problems. When he has mentioned children, you thought that he was talking about the distant future, after you move in together and get married, when you're in your mid-thirties maybe, with a career and a savings account. Part of you feels like when you are a real adult, your illness will disappear. You hate that Rowan looks unsatisfied with your reply. Jen laughs and says,

I forgot that you're so young. Rowan has always been desperate for sprogs. That was the problem.

Everybody laughs except Rowan, who looks down at his fish. Diane's laugh is especially loud, almost a cackle, and you think, I do not like any of these people. I want to go home. Diane shakes her head at Jen.

Don't say that. She'll think we're bitchy.

She turns to you,

Jane was always a big career woman. No time for mums like us.

You say,

What's wrong with that?

The silence is heavy, and then Jen says,

No, no. That's not what we meant.

The two women share a meaningful look. You suddenly

feel very tired. You can't believe that Rowan called Ella immature, and then brought you *here*. When you were in the taxi, a few hours before the dinner party, you felt nervous but also excited. Rowan had told you stories about being in uni with Jen and Diane. He said they were like you and Ella; always up for a night out, the last ones to leave the party. You imagined them accepting you into their confidence, including you in their jokes and making you feel wanted. You were looking forward to meeting them because you thought they might give you a glimpse into your and Ella's future, how your friendship would change and deepen as you got older. Sometimes, you imagined having a child at the same time as Ella, walking around the park together holding iced coffees and pushing identical buggies. You imagined throwing dinner parties like this one, but better, sneaking a cigarette in the garden while your partners chatted to each other and played with the kids. This evening has turned your fantasy sour. Maybe you and Ella are going to be like Diane and Jen in fifteen years; worn-out and bitter and tied to incompetent men who tell endless boring stories and don't help with the dishes. Maybe, you won't know each other at all.

Jen says, right, time to put Agnes down, and looks at her husband. Jonathon says, of course darling, and turns back to his conversation with Keir. Jen sighs, rolls her eyes, and stands up, peeling a sticky Agnes out of her highchair. Rowan asks if he can say goodnight to the baby, and you watch him get up and gently take her from Jen. He bends his head close to Agnes and kisses her on the forehead. His eyes look soft and happy, and he holds her easily, like she weighs nothing at all. The candlelight illuminates his shadow on the wall behind him and his elegant silhouette holding her small body looks almost holy. You feel a wave of emotion, mixed with wine, sweep through you. Agnes looks up at him, beaming, and then wipes her face on his clean shirt, leaving behind a mush of potato and sauce. Jen says, oh god I'm sorry, and reaches out to take her back, but Rowan laughs and says, it's not a problem. It'll come out in the wash. He looks at you and says, quietly, isn't she brilliant. You nod, and your throat feels tight. In that moment, you would give him anything he asked for. Jen takes Agnes back and asks Jonathon if he's going to say goodnight to his daughter. He pats Agnes on the head, and then wipes his hand on a napkin. When Jen goes upstairs, you hear the door slam. Agnes's cries echo back into the living room for a few minutes, but everybody ignores the noise.

An hour later, you've had sorbet and coffee and you are almost sober. It took Jen a while to get Agnes to sleep, and when she returned, she emptied the rest of a bottle of white wine into her glass, which still had a drop of red in it. The colours mixed, and she looked at you, and said, whoops. Now, Rowan is yawning, the other men are drunk, and you excuse yourself again. You make your way to the bathroom, but on your way, you change your mind. You slide open the deck door, go outside and light a cigarette. You strain your ears to hear cars, or people shouting, or any of the noises that you can usually hear from your flat on a Friday night, but everything is quiet and still. A burst of chatter rings out behind you, and you turn around and Rowan has slid the door open, so you can hear everyone inside. He comes to join you, and you give him your cigarette. He takes it and rests his head on your shoulder for a moment.

Shall we go soon?

You say,

Yes please.

Rowan smiles.

They aren't really my friends. Not anymore. Getting older changes people.

You nudge him.

You're old and you're still nice.

He says, cheeky, and blows smoke in your face. You head back inside, and when you're in the hallway, you hear Keir and Jonathon in the living room. You realise they're talking about you.

Rowan has done well for himself, hasn't he?

The two men laugh, and Keir replies,

Bit early for a mid-life crisis. But I'd rather have a go on her than buy a sports car.

You grab Rowan's arm to steady yourself, and when you look at him his face is red. Before you can say anything, you hear Jonathon say,

She's not much of a conversationalist. But I'm sure her mouth can do other things.

You assume that the women must be in a different room, but it is Diane who replies,

Poor Jane,

And it is the women who laugh the loudest. Rowan takes your hand and pulls you into the room. Everybody looks at you and you want to die. Jen says,

We didn't realise—

And Rowan waves his hand,

We're leaving anyway.

He starts to say something else, but you squeeze his hand and say, it doesn't matter, let's just go. Your voice breaks on the last word, and you know if you don't get out of the house immediately, you are going to cry. In the taxi home, Rowan apologises to you over and over again, and you say no really, it's fine, I don't care. He says,

I will never make you do that again.

He is so upset you think *he* is going to cry, so you say again that it's fine. You just want to be alone with him. When you get into bed, he holds you tight and says, I love you. I really love you, and you say, I know. I love you too.

The next morning, the two of you make an unspoken promise to pretend that the dinner party never happened. Rowan wakes you up with coffee and toast in bed and doesn't comment on the fact that you get crumbs all over the sheets. He is acting as if you have suffered a traumatic experience. You can't decide whether you view his behaviour as kindness or passivity. It is hard to decide what you wanted from him last night, if he could have done anything to make you feel better. You remember Douglas backing out of the hallway after the man on the train, Drew leaning in to kiss you at the club. Rowan's apology for his friends' behaviour, for the behaviour of men that you are forced to entertain, is hidden in the way he kisses you good morning, in the wonky, froth heart on top of the coffee. You find yourself thinking of Bertie, who would never have chosen to spend even a minute of her time in the company of Rowan's university friends, who would have overpowered Keir and Jonathon with her words, her knowledge, who wouldn't have even had to raise her voice to make them feel worthless. You know she would have fought for you, even if you asked her not to, but she wouldn't have held you close afterwards. Bertie's love did not leave room for softness, for complicated feelings. It grew from the same foundations as her personality and her politics, from anger. She loved you because you were a woman, because you were the same as her. She loved as a revolutionary act, a political choice, a fuck you to society. Rowan loves you in a way that feels separate from gender, politics, the world. He holds your hand; he takes you home. He didn't care that his friends were being sexist, he cared that they were hurting you. As you drink your coffee, you watch him pick your discarded clothes up off the floor, fold each item carefully, and stack them on the chair by the window. You think, that's how you love me. You wonder if it's how you want to be loved.

A&E

Rowan is driving you to work because you have a headache. You are staring at the window, silent, brittle, feeling like your skin is going to peel off if somebody touches you. You are burning hot, feverish, everything is too bright. Rowan reaches across and squeezes your knee. You jerk away. You know it isn't his fault that you are hormonal, but every fibre of your body is telling you that it *is* his fault, that you should lash out at him. You have felt like this for three days and you are worried that Rowan thinks you are going insane. He suggested you book a doctor's appointment and you told him to fuck off. He stops at a red light and you notice a missing cat poster stuck to a telephone pole. It is old, the edges are peeling. The cat is called Gus. You burst into tears and Rowan says, oh no, are you okay? You point at the poster, but the light turns green, and he starts to drive away. You are crying so hard you can't speak, and Rowan is glancing at you, then back to the road, then back to you. When you get to work, he can't find a parking space, so he just pulls up in front of the building, and you get out and slam the door before he can say goodbye. A split second after the door bangs shut, you crumple like a piece of paper, fainting straight onto the pavement, narrowly missing a broken bottle.

You come to lying across the backseat of Rowan's car, staring through the sunroof at the rain hitting the glass. Your vision is blurry and there is a boiling stone in the centre of your body. You turn your head to the side and throw up on the seat. You watch the thin mucus-y liquid drip onto the floor of the car. You hear Rowan say, fucking hell, but very far away, like he is down a tunnel. You feel like you are going faster and faster.

You wake up again when the car stops. Rowan opens the door beside your head, and you feel a cold rush of air and a smatter of rain on your face. Your mouth tastes like vinegar, and you can feel a partially dried line of fluid pasted from the side of your lip to your ear. He says, can you sit up? It's okay, I'm here. I'm lifting your head up, okay? Can you put your arms around me? And you manage to reach your arms in the direction of his voice. He half pulls, half lifts you out of the car, and you notice a smear of dark blood on the backseat.

You are leaning against Rowan; his arm is around your waist, your head is slumped forward, looking at your feet. Your trainers have sick on them, and you think, that is my sick. Rowan's shoes are so shiny, you can make eye contact with yourself in the sheen. He is shouting at a lady wearing scrubs, angrier than you have ever heard him. He says,

We can't fucking wait. Obviously, we can't fucking wait. Look at her.

The woman asks if you have any underlying health conditions and Rowan says, no, and you say yes, I do. Wait I do. You aren't sure if you are speaking out loud or inside your head.

The lady is pulling the curtain around the hospital bed you are lying on and you can hear someone moaning and

116

you think, can they shut up for one second, and then you realise it is you. You feel her place your feet into stirrups. You
realise that you are naked from the waist down. She says, how
long have you had the hormonal coil? And you say, I don't
know. She says, don't worry this won't take long, and then
she pulls something out of you like she is unplugging a sink
and you make a noise like an animal, and she says there you go.

Rowan is sitting next to you, holding your hand. He looks
old and tired. For a second you think, who is this man. You
deduce, from your woolly mouth and heaviness of your
limbs, that you have been given a sedative. You say, water,
and he hands you a paper cup. You reach out for it, and
misjudge the distance, your hand knocks against his. He
leans close to you with the cup, and you tilt your head
forward and drink. It is warm. You realise that he has been
crying. He bends forward and rests his forehead very gently
against your stomach for one second, and then sits back. He
says, thank god.

A doctor comes to speak to you. She tells you that your
body rejected the coil and attempted to expel it naturally.
Sometimes, this works. It's relatively unusual, but not
unheard of. People wake up one morning and find the small
T under their duvet or in their underwear. In your case, it
got stuck. The pain was unbearable, worsened by your
endometriosis. She was able to remove the device fully and
the displacement accounts for the pain and fever you have
been feeling for a few days. She does not know how long
the coil was in the wrong place, but this does reduce the
effectiveness of the device as a contraceptive and can possibly cause infection. She uses the phrase, foreign body, and

for a second, you think she means you, that she is acknowledging that your body is a stranger to you. You realise your mistake and you laugh. Rowan looks at you, confused. She says that she wants to keep you in overnight because she was concerned at the amount of blood you were losing. You realise that you are wearing a large pad, almost a nappy, and you wonder if Rowan was there when they put it on you.

When the two of you are alone, as alone as you can be in a public hospital ward, Rowan asks you why you didn't tell him what you were going through. You say, I don't know. Your thoughts are muddled, you are in pain, you don't want to have this conversation with him and ruin everything. You don't know that you're crying until you feel tears on your cheeks. Rowan scoots his chair closer and takes both of your hands in his. When he starts to speak, you wonder if he's been rehearsing what to say while you slept.

The doctor couldn't tell me much while you were asleep, but I heard her talking about endometriosis. I've been googling it. I've been wondering if you didn't tell me because you were afraid, but you don't have to be. I love you.

You nod, dazed, and say,

Sorry.

A few months before, you and Rowan had been lying in bed, talking about birthmarks. You showed him a collection of freckles on your stomach, and he tapped each one with the pad of his ring finger. His hand moved lower, brushing your surgery scar, right where the top of your underwear sat, and you tensed.

What is this?

Your stitches were long dissolved, but the scar is small, white and lumpy, a knot made out of skin. You have the same scar in your belly button, but nobody would notice it if they weren't looking, and the third incision, the one on the side of your abdomen, has faded away to nothing. You say,

I cut myself shaving.

He laughs and withdraws his hand.

That's a hell of a scar for a shaving mishap.

When Rowan comes to pick you up from the hospital the next morning, he is holding a bunch of flowers. The trousers you wore into the hospital are covered in blood, so you're wearing your work polo shirt with a pair of scrub trousers, and you have to keep pulling them up. You're also wearing hospital knickers and another postnatal pad. You haven't had a shower since the previous morning. He kisses your head and links his arm through yours. You don't know where you're going, so you let him steer you through the hospital corridors and out of the reception area into fresh air. The sky is grey and flat and it's raining. It feels like you haven't been outside in months. You let Rowan lead you to his car and as you get closer, you realise that Ella is sitting in the front seat. You tap on the window, and she looks up at you and smiles but you can tell that she isn't happy to see you. Rowan tells you to lie down across the backseat and goes to the boot to fetch you a blanket. Ella turns her head around, like your mother used to when you were kicking the back of her seat on long car journeys, and hisses, you didn't tell him? The drugs are wearing off, and you can feel the beginnings of a dull ache in your lower back and abdomen. You close your eyes and when Ella speaks again, you can tell that she's leaning close to you, so Rowan won't hear her while he fumbles about in the mess of the boot. You can feel her breath.

He called me. He was crying. I had to pretend that I didn't know. I had to *lie.*

You whisper that you're sorry, but your voice is muffled by the sound of the boot closing. You open your eyes and watch Rowan get into the front seat. He turns his head back and says, okay? And you nod. You drift in and out of sleep on the way home, listening to the quiet buzz of Ella and Rowan's conversation, unable to make out the words. When you open your eyes, you look up at the backs of their heads and they look like strangers.

Bellahouston again

Rowan is sitting next to you on the sofa, his computer on his lap. You are trying to read, holding a cold glass of white wine against your hot forehead. You can't focus on the words on the page, so you keep looking over at him, feeling more and more irritated by the way he hunches over the laptop and types with two fingers. He keeps angling the screen to show you photos of people you do not know or care about, and saying inane things like, Sophie's daughter is seven already! I remember when she was born.

It's been over a month since the coil came out, but the cramping and bleeding hasn't gone away, and Rowan is worried about you. You have tried to explain that this is normal, that the waxing and waning of your pain is unpredictable and you just have to ride it out. You can tell that he is unsatisfied with this, and he thinks you should try something new for the pain or get a second opinion. He does research and comes back to you with printed out articles and studies on experimental treatments. He calls a doctor friend and asks him if there's anyone you can be referred to, an endometriosis specialist or someone in the private sector. You know that he is doing it out of love, but whenever he hands you his annotated articles or sends you a podcast to listen to, all you hear is him saying, try harder. You aren't willing to talk about your condition with him and even if you were, you don't know how to tell him how you feel without coming across as unattractive or bitter. A couple of times in the past month, he has tried to discuss having children, and you have tried to explain that you can't even think about it right now, that all your energy is devoted to treading water and if you stop to think about anything, you'll sink. He tells you that he wants to be with you forever, that you'll figure out a way to have children, that he'll help you find a job that can work around your illness. He picks up your hand and you force yourself not to pull away. It's the same every time and his serious expression makes you feel like you are dying. The hospital visit has brought down a wall between the two of you that you had put there on purpose, and now you resent his closeness, his questions. You miss the days where the functions of your individual bodies were unknown to each other, when it would be unthinkable for him to ask you about your period, about your blood. When you have sex, he is so gentle that it makes your skin crawl. He asks you if you're okay, he never initiates. When he touches you, you can barely feel it. You know that he doesn't want you anymore, that your shine has gone away. You used to be his young, hot girlfriend who loved his house and his cooking, and now you are damaged goods. He wants to protect you from harm, cure your incurable illness, keep you in his house where you can't get hurt. You make him fuck you even when you can tell he doesn't want to. You move his hands to your breasts, your hips, your throat. Afterwards, when he tries to hold you close and whisper things in your ear, you turn away.

*   *   *

You are still taking the painkillers that the doctor gave you and they make you slow and stupid. You make several small mistakes at work, attend a disciplinary, get denied paid time off and finally quit. Ella takes you out for lunch on your last day, and you push a tomato back and forth on your plate while she tells you she's sorry and offers to try and find you something new. You leave the café before she's finished eating, let her handle the bill and ignore her follow up texts asking if you're okay. Since then, you have been spending your days sleeping late, dosing up on medication and floating around Rowan's house. He says that you're recovering, but you feel like an unhappy housewife, waiting for him to come home so you can suggest you open a bottle of wine or smoke a joint. Your savings are dwindling, he is paying for all your food, and you owe Ella's parents a month of rent. Your life is suspended, confined to the walls of the house that you used to love, where you are constantly reminded of Rowan's kindness and your incompetence. You have no idea what you are going to do, but you are constantly struck by the urge to do something. You wake up in the middle of the night, you try to write or apply for jobs, but you never finish anything. Your pain is low level but constant and it dulls your senses until you are incapable of making even simple decisions about what you want for dinner or what to watch on TV. You have been thinking about language, about how hard it is for you to express your feelings through words. You begin texts to Ella, and then hit the backspace key on your phone until the message is blank. When she contacts you, you reply with one word or ignore the message.

*   *   *

Rowan picks up his laptop for the third time in ten minutes, to show you a picture of Janine, his administrative assistant at the university. He is fond of her and mentions her often.

Look, that's Janine,

he says, pointing to a picture of a middle-aged woman wearing a dress with flowers on it. She is pregnant, but not far along, you wouldn't be able to tell if she wasn't cradling the bump with her hands. You say, okay, and look back at your book. You've read the same sentence three times. You are bristling at his kindness, his preoccupations with other people's families. You give up, put the book down and scooch closer to him to look at the picture properly. He angles the screen so you can see it better, happy that you're joining in. You point at her dress and wrinkle your nose, saying,

Ew, what is she wearing?

Don't be unkind.

Rowan moves away from you, so you can't see the picture anymore. Your laptop privileges have been revoked. You watch him scroll and click, scroll, and click. You think that he would stay with you forever, even if you continued behaving like this. You know that if you were talking to Ella, she would tell you how to fix things, remind you that you are lucky to be with someone who wants to build a future with you. You are so tired of disappointing people. You remember what she said to you when you came back from Aberdeen, the way her voice shook when she asked you to stop doing this. You know that you are about to make a mistake, you know it with a clarity that you haven't possessed in months, but you can't stop yourself. You say, Rowan? And when he looks up at you, you tell him that it's done, and you don't change your mind, not even when he cries, or kisses you, or throws your shoes across the hallway when you're about to leave. You don't change your mind until you're on the train back into town, back to your flat that you haven't been to in over a month, back to Ella, who isn't speaking to you, and is going to be so sad when you tell her what you've done.

Clinic

The topic of Rowan hangs between you and Ella and your conversations become passive-aggressive and shallow. She told her parents about your situation, and they agreed to waive your rent while you get back on your feet, but you are still unable to finish a job application. Every week when your bank texts you your balance, the slowly decreasing number makes you feel ill.

This year, Ella decides to take Will home to the cottage for Christmas. When she tells you her plans, her tone is light, but she doesn't look you in the eye, and you can tell that she thinks you're going to take it badly. You don't care. The sense of aimlessness that trapped you inside Rowan's house has followed you back to the flat, and you continue to waste the days sleeping and smoking and scrolling, ignoring Ella's emails with links to job adverts and whiteboard reminders to take the bin out. When she goes down south, you don't miss her. It's easier to exist without her presence tying you to reality, so when she's gone, you detach completely.

Eventually, you run out of painkillers and when you try to refill the prescription, the pharmacist tells you that it hasn't been approved for repeat use. You make a note to call the doctor, but don't follow up, so you withdraw from the medication alone in the flat, throwing up every morning and falling asleep on the sofa from exhaustion, waking up fourteen hours later with a dry mouth and sore head. The symptoms don't go away after a few days, so you call the NHS helpline, and when the woman on the other end of the phone asks if you've missed a period you laugh. You tell her that the reason you were taking the painkillers in the first place was to help with endometriosis pain after a coil removal, and when she asks what contraception you've been using since then, everything comes into sickeningly sharp focus. You hang up and open the bathroom cabinet, rifling through plasters and UTI medication until you find a multipack of tests that Ella bought a few years ago. You think about calling her while you wait for the test to develop, but then you imagine her and Will drinking wine in the living room of the cottage and decide not to bother. When the two positive lines develop on the test, you are alone, and the flat is quiet except for distant shouts and city noises drifting up through the window from the street. It feels anti-climactic because you already know. You put the test in the bin and walk into the kitchen where you wash your hands and boil the kettle. While your tea is brewing, you try not to dwell on the irony of this fucking situation you've managed to get yourself in, and instead you do a quick Google search and then make a phone call.

*

Two days before Christmas Eve, you go to the sexual health clinic. It's early in the morning, the sun isn't quite up yet and you're surprised that the stretch of street outside is quiet and empty. You have been staying up late reading articles about pro-life protesters and religious fanatics, and you were worried that somebody was going to be here to shout at you, to try and draw attention to what you're about to do. You wonder if you had wanted that to happen, to be punished so that you can feel the weight of your decision. The ease with which you have navigated the past few days surprises you, that as soon as you decided what to do, you felt better, and were able to think about other things. Now the only negative feeling is the niggling thought that has sat inside your head for years now; the knowledge that there is something wrong with you, that you are lacking some part of your brain that makes you care about your own choices or the things that happen to you. Another reason for your surprise at the empty pavement was that you were expecting, wanting, to see Ella waiting for you outside. That despite the distance and lack of communication, you believed that she would have been able to sense what was happening and come to sit with you in the waiting room like she has done so many times before.

The receptionist is kind to you, and so is the nurse who shows you into an examination room and tells you that the doctor will be with you in just a minute. When the doctor arrives, she talks you through the procedure, gives you the first tablet to take orally, and then hands you a paper bag full of medications and extra-large pads. She tells you to call the number on the packet if you have any problems and make sure that you get lots of rest. You have to pretend that someone is picking you up and staying with you for the next twenty-four hours, so in a fit of fantasy, you tell the doctor that your boyfriend is sitting outside in the car. She smiles and says, make sure he looks after you, and you nod. You have an urge to confess then, to tell her that you're lying, that you don't have a boyfriend anymore, that you left him, and he doesn't even know that you're here. That if you called him right now and told him that you were pregnant, he would be happy. But then she wouldn't let you leave, so you just walk home alone and sit on your bathroom floor in the dark, staring at the paper bag.

The information packet tells you to take an anti-sickness tablet and some painkillers, wait twenty minutes, eat something, and then insert the final three tablets vaginally. You were given the option to insert the suppositories in the clinic, but you felt embarrassed at the thought of touching yourself in the public bathroom. You have just removed the three oval tablets from their packaging and lined them up in front of you when your phone buzzes. A text message from your mother reads When is your train getting in? and you ignore it. You google early pregnancy, and learn that, at that very moment, the thing inside of you is growing optic vesicles, which will later turn into eyeballs. A comment on the article says that the heart might have already started beating. You do not care. You feel so disconnected from whatever is inside of you that you find it impossible to imagine that if you left it alone, it would turn into a human that was half you and half Rowan. The heartbeat, or lack thereof, feels like none of your business.

You take the pills and wash them down with some warm water from the kitchen tap. Then you spread your legs as wide as they go and insert the capsules without looking at yourself too closely. You feel the thick tablets shift uncomfortably inside you and you start to feel sick. You are acutely aware of your own body, the sweat cooling on your arms, between your toes. When you swallow, your tongue feels like it is getting bigger and bigger, almost choking you, a wet animal inside your mouth. You wish for the happy oblivion of being high, of being drunk, of escaping yourself. The doctor explained that the bleeding would start quickly and wouldn't be much heavier than your regular periods, since it was early on. You thought about telling her that you don't have regular periods but didn't want to be difficult. When she asked if you had ever experienced any kind of sexual trauma, you said, no, um, I don't know, and she said, are you sure? And you shook your head.

You didn't switch on any of the lights when you came home, and the winter light is weak, so the flat is dark and unwelcoming. You feel a dull ache at the very bottom of your stomach and then the blood starts. You get into the bath and run the hot tap on full and try to distract yourself by thinking about something else. You focus your eyes very intensely on the various toiletries on the edge of the bath, Ella's mint shampoo, Ella's lavender shower gel. You don't want to think of her, so your close your eyes tight and sink back into the steaming water, enveloping yourself until you can't feel your own body anymore. You allow yourself to imagine what would happen if you had missed your appointment, if you moved back in with Rowan and redecorated, creating a perfect home that fit both of your tastes perfectly. You see tiny shoes and sleepsuits, the spare room painted pink or blue. You create a blissful nine months for yourself full of rom-com worthy scenes that culminate with Rowan getting down on one knee and promising that he will love you forever. In the fantasy, you are someone else, someone more like Ella, who accepts goodness into her life with the air of someone who deserves it. Even in your imagination, you cannot envision yourself giving birth, inflicting even more trauma on the body that has always failed you. The cramps get sharper, more insistent, but you are used to pain like this. After an hour or so, you feel strong enough to get out of the bath, clean up the mess and go to bed. You sleep the rest of the day and wake up in the middle of the night, feverish and sticky. You've bled through your underwear and onto the sheets, so you get up and change. You take the bedding to the washing machine but in the end, you just throw it away, like you're disposing of evidence. You don't have enough energy to remake the bed, so you cover the mattress with an old towel and lie down, pressing your forehead against the cool pillow. When you close your eyes, sparks of colour dance across the back of your eyelids and you cannot collect your thoughts. When you next wake, it's early morning and the fever has broken. You check your phone and see that you texted Ella a few hours ago, I'm sorry I've been so weird can I ring you tomorrow? I love you. You don't remember sending the message. In the shower, you watch a consistent line of thin pinkish blood run down your leg and swirl into the drain. You stay under the hot water for half an hour and when you get out, you feel clean.

Home

Your mum is waiting in the car park, and you can tell that she is annoyed before you even open the door. The train was delayed by twenty minutes and the first thing she says to you, the first thing she has said to you in person in almost a year, is,

You're late.

The train was delayed.

That's what happens when you decide to travel on Christmas Eve.

You're both silent for the next five minutes, competing to see who will give in and talk first. Your stomach hurts and you're still bleeding but the discomfort is manageable, nothing you haven't tolerated before. Ella hasn't texted you back yet and you can't stop looking at your phone even though it is on loud. You can tell that your constant checking is annoying your mum, the way you keep picking it up and putting it down, and after a few minutes she speaks, losing the game,

Do you have to keep doing that?

You put the phone face down on your knee and take a deep breath of stale air. The windshield wipers cut back and forth uselessly. It's barely spitting. Mum sighs and presses a button on the dashboard and a hymn rings out of the radio, too loud in the overheated car. *It is the night of our dear saviour's birth, long lay the world in sin and error pining, til he appeared, and the soul felt its world.* You turn it off and look out the window and both of you remain silent for the rest of the drive. When you get back to the house, you get out as soon as the car stops, run up the driveway and open the front door before your mum has even switched off the engine. You kick your shoes off and pull your bag into the hallway. She follows you in and puts her own shoes pointedly onto the small shoe rack by the front door. You look at the rack, which only has four pairs of shoes on it: Mum's smart heels, Mum's trainers, Mum's everyday plimsolls, Dad's boots. You remember having a row just for your own shoes when you were a child, and it occurs to you that when you moved out, they must have bought a new rack with only two shelves. You get a cold, tight feeling in your throat, like you're trying to swallow an ice cube. The house is cold and pristine and apart from the rack, you don't notice any differences. You head down the hallway into the kitchen and Mum pushes past you to go to the sink and wash her hands.

She tells you to shower and then check in with your dad. You put your bags in your bedroom, which your mum calls the guest room. The room bares no trace of your childhood; the NME posters and charcoal sketches have been taken down and the chest of drawers is empty. You wonder where your clothes are; vacuum packed in a cupboard somewhere or sent off to the charity shop? You try and figure out how many times you've been here since you moved. Maybe twice, maybe three times, never for more than two nights. It's like you're afraid that if you stay for too long, you won't be able to leave. You don't feel real when you're here, and as soon as you get back to Glasgow, you try and erase everything that happened from your mind. Ella had long learned not to ask questions. You sit on the bathroom floor and run the shower while you reread the text. You feel stupid.

After five minutes or so you flick water on a towel until it's damp and hang it up on the radiator because you know she'll check. You open the door to the living room and say hi to your dad, who is sitting in his armchair and watching football. He's holding a beer and empty bottles circle his feet. If you had to paint a portrait of your father, this is the scene you would choose. The back of the green chair, his bald head poking over the top, the light emanating from the oversized TV screen and making the rest of the room dark. He starts at your interruption, and you walk deeper into the room and sit on the edge of the sofa facing him. You look at the timeline of your school pictures on the wall and try to remember who you were when they were taken, how you felt at twelve, fourteen, seventeen. You watch your father watching the screen and wonder if he ever turns his head to the left and looks at the photographs of you, if he thinks about where you are and what you're doing. He looks old and tired, his clothes ill-fitting and so obviously picked out by Mum, his face red from a lifetime of beers and fatty food. He tears his eyes away from the screen and gives you a quick once over, nodding hello before looking back at the TV. In a low voice he asks, you alright? And you say that you are. You watch the game together in silence for a few seconds and then you leave the room.

You sit at the kitchen table and watch Mum do the dishes. You know that she wants you to offer to help, and that when you do, she will take pleasure in refusing. The silence is paining you, but you are feeding it, nonetheless. You remember the games you used to play when you lived here, the sulking and pouting and arguments that she always won. You force yourself to ask what her plans are for the evening, and she points at the door to the downstairs living room. You remember being proud of the fact that your parents had two living rooms when you were a child because you thought it was a sign of wealth. But now you're older, you realise that you cannot recall a single evening in which your parents watched TV together, or even ate dinner in the same room. Mum returns the question without turning around or inviting you to join her and you say, I'm going out. She says, yes, in a tight voice and you watch her straight back and the muscles in her arms as she scrubs. You say, have a good evening, and she makes a non-committal noise, a kind of hmm sound. You clench your hands into fists to fight a sudden urge to slam them on the table. You want to stay and talk to her; you want to try. You grab your coat and scarf and step out into the cold air before you stop to think about where you're going.

When you walk into the pub, the warmth overwhelms you and you immediately start sweating. You look around, taking stock of the tables, and notice an old man, still wearing his coat and hat, staring into the bottom of his pint glass. You wonder if it's the same guy who used to hang about when you lived here, getting drunker and drunker and trying it on with the teenage girls. All old men look the same to you; their sad beige jackets and yellow tipped fingers. You pray that your dad has never done this, remembering how he always let his gaze rest on the prettiest friend at your sleepovers. You manage to banish the thought before it sticks. There are no tables free, and you scan the room, avoiding the judgemental gaze of the regulars, until you see

Duncan. You went to primary school together and had established a relationship of convenience for a few years because you both preferred reading in the corner of the playground to flinging balls around and skipping. Without discussion, you developed a routine of sharing your packed lunches, divvying up the spoils and making your way through them methodically, starting with the best; Peperami and Frubes, and leaving the fruit until last. Duncan's lunches were always superior, full of branded snacks and supermarket sandwich fillings, whereas yours were packed in a hurry by yourself after your parents had left for work. He never mentioned it. You didn't speak in high school, but sometimes he smiled at you in the corridors. He became cool, probably because he was quick to laugh and had an older brother who occasionally bought him vodka. You ran in different circles. You lost track of him when you left, but he looks the same. It's only when you get closer that you see; he's softer now and his hair is longer. He's sitting with a group of boys that you also recognise from the periphery of your childhood. Findlay and Ally. When did you come here last? The summer before uni, maybe the day you left school.

Duncan looks up from his drink and notices you. You wave and he smiles and beckons you over. When the rest of the group realise who you are, they start shouting and hugging you as if they've really missed you. Findlay jumps up to buy you a drink without asking what you want and the rest of the boys shuffle around the booth to make space for you. Duncan asks what you've been doing, and you shrug and say, I'd rather hear about you. They tell you where they're working (in or around the town), who they're getting with (girls from school), where they're living (with their parents). The basics are covered in a few sentences and after they're finished Findlay sums it up by saying, so fuck all, basically. Duncan stays quiet, watching you, and his gaze makes you feel even warmer. You look back at him and smile and he says, quietly, aside from the main conversation, you've gone red, are you hot? You nod and he picks up your beer and holds the bottle against your forehead, gently. The icy glass makes you breathe in quickly and you say, that feels good. You are pulled back into the conversation by Findlay asking you how long you're home for and you shrug and say probably just a day or two. Ally shakes his head and says, you have to stay Boxing Day night, we're going out, it's always mad. You ask where they're going and he gestures around the room as if to say, where else? These boys have been here, drinking in the same pub, kissing the same girls, while you moved away and forgot all about them. Your expression must betray you because Ally looks down and says defensively, it's good, it's really good. You say, yeah it sounds fun, but privately, you pity him. Being home fills you with a sense of superiority that you rarely feel when you're in Glasgow. You know you're struggling, but you're still better than this.

In the space of an hour, you get drunk, drunker than everyone else. Maybe because you rarely drink beer or maybe because you feel so unbelievably relieved to be doing something normal, to be drinking in the pub with boys from school who don't know a thing about how you've been living for the past seven years. You are talking and talking, more than you usually do, forgetting what you've said before the words have fully escaped your mouth. It is liberating to paint yourself a new personality because the voice inside your head that usually judges and demeans you has been dulled in the face of your drunkenness. The dim lights in the pub that looked cheap when you entered have become an addition that makes the room warm and comforting. The dust on the bar is charming now, the smudged glass in front of you full of character. You know when you wake up tomorrow you will have forgotten all of this, that your body will become bloated with anxiety and paranoia. You will rack your brain for details of the ways in which you embarrassed yourself, but the memories won't come, so you'll invent things that you did that are even worse than what happened. You want to remember this evening the way it feels right now, even better than reality. You take your phone out and write a few lines of prose describing the scene and when Duncan asks you what you're doing you say, I'm a writer, with no sense of deprecation or irony. Basking in the full strength of his approval, the lie sounds true.

You and Duncan go outside for a cigarette, sheltering from the rain under the gazebo that covers the beer garden. You wish it was snowing instead, white feathery flakes that would land on your faces and tongues and evaporate into nothing. It's late now, almost last call, almost Christmas Day. You ask Duncan how his mum is and say that you still remember her from when you were kids. You can't picture her face, but you remember her laugh at the school gates, the notes in Duncan's lunchbox. You remind him of your food trades, thinking it will make him laugh, but he gives you a look that you can't interpret. He takes a breath, like he's psyching himself up to speak. When he replies, the words come out forced, but like he's trying to sound relaxed.

Oh, she died.

God, I'm sorry. I didn't realise.

You wonder why your mum never told you this, or maybe she did and you just didn't care. Duncan shrugs,

It's okay. I feel fine about it.

It occurs to you, a sober thought drifting across your drunk mind, that this is a strange thing to say, but you can't think of anything comforting to do, so you just blow cigarette smoke in his face and say, do you want to get shots? When you go back inside, Ally is slumped at your table, maybe asleep or maybe passed out, and Findlay is flirting with the girl on the bar. You remember her. She was your neighbour. You grab Duncan's arm,

Why is Findlay trying to get with her? She's so young.

Duncan says,

Who? Eilidh? She's twenty.

You remember watching her learning to ride a bike from your front window, her dad picking her up when she fell. You watch Duncan go and order your drinks and she smiles at him before she turns around. She's flirting, she's pretty. When you tip your head back and drain the tequila, the liquid burns your throat and makes your eyes water. You put the glass on the bar, too hard, and ignore Eilidh when she asks how you're doing.

By the time the pub closes, you are almost too drunk to stand. You are leading the conversation now, leaning heavily against the sticky bar, laughing at your own jokes. You can sense that you're going on and on, that you're boring everyone. Eilidh is ringing a bell and flicking the lights on and off to rush everyone out, but the noise and changing brightness barely registers to you, because you are focusing all your energy on finishing your long and meandering story, which follows you and Ella on a raucous girls' holiday to Berlin. The story is fictional, so you're still trying to figure out how it ends. Duncan fetches your coat and tells you to hold your arms out so he can put it on for you. He loops your scarf around your neck and pulls your hair out of your collar. You want to kiss him, but you feel sick, so you don't, and while you're trying to quell the nausea the boys decide to go back to Duncan's house for afters because his dad is on holiday with his girlfriend. It's still raining hard, so you and Duncan start to run, the other boys behind you, silhouettes in the dark. As you turn onto the high street, the pavement slopes downwards and you speed up, running as fast as you can, your wet hand slipping out of Duncan's, sideways rain hitting your face so hard you feel like it's going to leave a mark. You are exhilarated, you are laughing but nobody can hear you in the storm. You get to his house first, your feet leading you there without instruction even though you haven't been there in over a decade. You stand in the doorway trying not to shiver as the rain seeps through your clothes. You check your phone, squinting your eyes to try and focus on the blurry text on the screen. You ignore a message from your mum that reads: going to bed and look at the time instead. Past midnight. 25 Dec. You remember a Christmas when you were seven or eight, writing a long list unbeknown to your parents, and slipping it into the postbox on the walk to school, addressed to Mr Santa Claus, North Pole. You stole stamps from your mum's kitchen drawer and stuck four of them on the white envelope with your gluey saliva. When Christmas morning came, you ran down to the living room and checked underneath the plastic tree for your gifts. After ripping through the presents from your parents, you sat back on your haunches and cried hot wet tears that made your pyjama collar damp and your head sore. Your mum found you there, weeping amongst the ripped paper, and there was a screaming argument at breakfast, over premixed Buck's Fizz, about how ungrateful you were, about how hard they had worked to afford these presents and how rude it was to open them before they'd even got up. You, still crying, choking on every word, tried to explain that you weren't upset about the presents, you were upset that Santa didn't care about you. Your mum sat back for a moment, stunned, and then she started to laugh. Dad joined in, and after the amusement faded, breakfast was resumed. You cried even harder because you didn't understand why they were laughing. Remembering this feeling now, you feel the same ache in your head, the same blooming wetness behind your eyes. You wish they had cared enough to pretend. You can't even remember what you wanted.

When the boys catch up, Duncan struggles to stop his hand from shaking long enough to fit his key in the lock. As you all spill into the hall, soaked through and beginning to lose steam, Duncan turns the heating on high, puts music on and finds you all clean clothes. You get undressed in front of each other like kids in a football changing room, trying not to look at each other's wet bodies. You're wearing Duncan's leavers hoodie and you twist to look at your back in the mirror, scanning the mass of tiny, printed names until you find your own. You resolve to find your own hoodie when you get back, until you remember the empty drawers. You head into the living room and turn the music up louder while Ally goes to search for booze. He comes in a minute later, triumphant, arms full of half-empty bottles. He lays them out side by side on the carpet like bodies and you pick one each to swig from. You feel like a child, drinking someone's parents' vodka, wearing someone else's hoodie, and listening to remixes from the 2010s. You wish you were at the cottage with Ella and her parents, tucked up in the spare room with *Little Women* to read if you can't sleep. Duncan asks if you're okay and you aren't sure what to say. Before you get a chance to make something up, Findlay saves the day.

Merry Christmas kiddies,

he says too loudly, grinning and pulling a baggie out of his backpack.

You split a pill with Duncan and later, maybe hours later, you go into the garden and notice his trampoline. There's a safety net surrounding the nylon circle, so you have to unzip the netting to climb inside. Duncan zips it back up behind you, so you feel enclosed and safe lying on your back and looking straight up at the black sky. The sensation of rain on your face feels incredible, soft and tickly and not even cold anymore. You smack your palm against the sodden trampoline and the rain flies up around your hand. You say, it's like Michael playing the keyboard with the M&Ms, and Duncan says, what? without sitting up or opening his eyes. You try again, poking him in the side, and say, in *The Princess Diaries*? He shakes his head, eyes still closed. For a second you feel groundlessly disappointed in Duncan and think of Ella, who would have understood this reference and laughed. At that very moment, almost as if you have manifested it, Ella texts you back. You have to hold the phone right up to your face and squint your eyes to make out the message, and in doing so you notice the time. You realise how late it is, that Ella must be drunk too. You are having fun here, with this boy who likes you, but you would rather be with her, always. She's written, happy christmas!! we can talk soon. Xxxxx

Fog drifts across the moon and it gets so dark you can hardly make out Duncan's features. You sit up and look into the window that leads to the living room. Findlay and Ally are sitting on the floor, framed by the window. They look like actors in a sitcom with the volume turned way down; you can't hear them, but you can tell that they're laughing by their faces. Duncan says, can I tell you something, and you nod, but he isn't looking at you, so he says, hey, can I? You say, yeah, out loud this time, and he says, I fancied you in school. You don't know what to say in reply because you know it isn't true, but maybe he believes it now because you're lying here together, high and drunk and looking at the moon. You turn onto your side, and he turns to face you and you say, really? and he says, yeah, and then he kisses you and you kiss him back. His lips feel the same as the rain, your mouth tingles and you feel yourself getting turned on, the knot in your stomach tightens and you put one hand in his hair and pull.

You go back into the house through the side door and run up the stairs. The music is so loud compared to the silence of outside that it feels like it's coming from inside of you. You pause at the top of the stairs and say, where's your bedroom? And Duncan points at a door, identical to the others in the hallway, but when you open it, you find yourself in a small bathroom. Duncan slides the bolt across to lock the door and brushes past you to put the shower on. He turns back to kiss you and starts to peel his wet clothes away from your body. He pulls the hoodie over your head and holds both of your hands so you can step out of his joggers. He stands in front of you, fully clothed, looking at you, and you fold your arms across your chest. He pulls them away and kisses the space between your breasts, right down to your belly button. You remember, almost too late, the bulky pad in your underwear, the blood, and you put your hands on his head and gently pull him up to face you. You kiss him and say, I'm on my period, sorry, and he says it's okay and takes off his jumper. In the shower, the steam makes you dizzy, and you can't get under the jet of water properly, so you are too cold and too hot at the same time. You are both naked now, pressed against each other, kissing and touching and laughing when he gets water in his eyes, or you slip a little on the linoleum. You hope Duncan hasn't noticed that you're still bleeding. You don't really want him anymore, but you feel comfortable. You keep remembering his face as a child, the way his glasses would steam up when he tucked his chin inside his jumper. You wonder what his big brother is doing now, you want to ask, but you can't remember his name and it feels like the wrong time anyway. After a while, you start to shiver, and Duncan asks if you want to get out. You nod and he turns the shower off and wraps you in a towel that smells like it hasn't dried properly. You hang back in the bathroom and put your underwear on, so you don't bleed onto his sheets. You get into bed together and you can feel your wet hair soaking through his pillow. You lie facing each other again, like on the trampoline, and kiss for another few minutes before Duncan pulls away and says, I'm really tired, aren't you? And you shake your head. Your heart is beating so fast you're surprised he can't hear it and your head is starting to hurt. You roll onto your back and Duncan snuggles into you, pressing his head into the space between your neck and collarbone, yawning into your skin. You stare at the ceiling, waiting for his breathing to slow and dreading the moment that you will become alone. You move your hand to touch him, stroking gently until he gets hard, and then speeding up, kissing his neck and whispering things that are supposed to sound sexy. His eyes are closed, his mouth is open slightly, but he angles his hips towards your touch. You sit up and straddle his thigh, bending down and putting your mouth on him. You hate doing this, you always have, but you want to prolong the night, you want him to stay with you. When it is over, you move up his body to kiss him and he gives you his cheek and rolls onto his side, making space for you next to him in the rumpled sheets. Within minutes, he is asleep. You wait as long as you can, counting your heart-beats, making up stories in your head, trying to empty your mind of thoughts. You feel bad. You feel bad. You feel bad. After a while, you check your phone, and it is almost 5am. You extract yourself from Duncan's sleeping body and wrap the towel back around yourself. You retrace your steps back down the stairs and find your clothes, which are dry now, on the radiator. Ally has disappeared and Findlay is asleep on the sofa in the living room, so you dress quietly and slip out the front door. The rain has stopped, and the street is deserted. Your headphones have died, so you walk in silence without a single car passing you. You make a wrong turn and double back on yourself, the sky is black and opaque. This is your hometown, but you feel like there are things lurking in the shadows, that if you stop and look for too long, they will take shape, become solid. But then, thankfully, the spare key is still in a small safe attached to the side of the house and the code is still your mum's birthday. You get into bed fully clothed, aware of the smoke in your hair, the stale sweat on your back and armpits, the bad taste in your mouth. You lie there, motionless, for hours with the blind open, watching the shadows of the blowing trees on the wall. When you fall asleep, the sun is rising, and when you wake up, it is midday. You can smell the turkey.

Wales

My grandmother died.

It is early morning, 2nd January, still dark. You are hungover, alone, reeling at the sound of Ella's voice on the end of the line, a voice that you knew better than your own but has, in the last few weeks, become alien to you. She says your name and it sounds like a question and you don't know what to say, so you just open your mouth and let words fall out, hoping that they are reassuring.

Oh god, oh no, what happened?

And she starts to explain, her voice thick with tears, trailing off every few words to inhale and exhale deeply. She tells you that her grandmother had a brain aneurysm in the early hours of New Year's Day. She had gone to bed just after midnight and Ella and Will stayed up, sitting in the living room, drinking prosecco, and talking about their resolutions. She stops talking and you hear Will's voice in the background, his soothing voice saying it's okay, it's okay, and you think, of course he's there, being perfect. Ella comes back to the phone and starts again,

I'm sorry, I just feel so stupid. We were drunk, I thought she came down to ask us to be quiet. She was wearing her nightgown and she said her head hurt. She just—

You start to cry too. You are troubled by the pain in Ella's voice, how unequipped you are to help her, to make her feel better. There's a rustling on the other end and the next voice you hear is Will's.

Hi. Ella's given me the phone,

Hey.

You feel embarrassed of your tears. You don't want him to think that you are performing, making this about you.

Ella wanted to tell you straight away. We're going to stay here for a few days, sort everything out. Ian and Christine are coming. I have to go back to work on the fourth and Ella was wondering—

He takes a deep breath, as if he is choosing his words carefully.

She was wondering if you would come to Wales for a few days. Do you think you could do that?

You hear the warning in his voice, the things he wants to say but can't with Ella listening. Don't fuck this up. Don't let her down again. You wipe your nose with your hand and sit up like he can see you.

Yes. I'll come. I'll be there.

You catch the train on the fifth of January and spend the journey thinking about Ella, wondering how you can support her, hoping that this is a chance for you to even the scales of your relationship. You have no idea how to feel, or what it's going to be like to see her. In the days between your phone call and the train, you have barely spoken to her, except to confirm travel logistics and ask her periodically how she is. She has been uncharacteristically blunt in her replies, and you have no idea what kind of scene you will be arriving to. You wonder how you would feel in her position but know that it's incomparable. During every period of familial mourning, your dad's lost job, your mother's depression, the deaths of your own faraway grandparents, you experienced an uncontrollable urge to put as much distance between you and your family as you possibly could.

Moving out for university was a blessing; your mother would update you on family news sporadically by text and then, when you didn't reply, not at all. When your gran died in your first year of uni, a brittle chain-smoker you met three times, you didn't go to the funeral. It didn't feel monumental then; you didn't grieve or worry about how your dad would cope. Looking back at the timeline of your relationship with your parents, the funeral could be pinpointed as the moment in which your life line diverged from theirs. Going home for Christmas was stupid, the pathetic misstep of someone high on painkillers and plagued by intermittent feelings of sentimentality. Part of you – and you know this now – thought that it wasn't too late to put a plaster over everything, that going home with the experience and insight of a twenty-six-year-old was all you needed to heal. When you finally surfaced on Christmas day, visibly hungover, your mother refused to look at you, addressing your congealing plate instead of you directly. You gave your parents their gifts, which had seemed tasteful and kind at the time of purchase but viewed through the dull haze of a comedown and your mother's pessimism, they looked cheap and sad. You got the first bus to the station on Boxing Day without waking your parents up. When Duncan messaged you, you blocked him. You spent the week in between Christmas and New Year's Eve alone in the flat, trying to read Proust again, and when you failed, resorting to crime thriller novels and red wine from the corner shop.

As the train pulls into Cardiff station, it occurs to you that you are in a new country, that you have no idea what to expect. You take your headphones off and, overwhelmed by the reintroduction of noise, stumble onto the platform. It's freezing cold and dark, early evening. You could be anywhere. Ian is a few minutes late and when you get into the front seat of the car, it smells like cigarettes and something else you can't place that reminds you of the dentist. He reaches out to pat you on the shoulder and says, been a while hasn't it, and you nod, and wish that you could lean over to hug him without it being weird. You wish that he was driving you to the cottage, and he could continue to fulfil the role that you have given him and Christine, which is to make you feel like everything in the world is easier to take. You know that this time things are different, and you don't get to be the one who is suffering.

Ella wipes her undereye roughly with her pointer finger and pulls her jumper down over her hands like she's cold. She picks up her mug and puts it down again, goes to get sugar then shuts the cupboard without taking any out. She's making your tea wrong, adding cow's milk, forgetting the honey. You want to help but you don't know where anything is in the house, which is unbearably warm and filled with clutter and dust. You are a spare part. Ella clicks the kettle on and turns around to face you.

Dad's been awful, as you can imagine. Mum's been doing the practical stuff, but she's gone home now, and I feel like I've just been looking after him, hovering. I haven't had a minute to think—

Her voice wobbles.

To think about her. To feel sad for myself.

Why don't you go back to Glasgow? Or to the cottage, to see Christine. It can't be good for you being here.

Ella's face tells you that you have said the wrong thing.

I can't do that. The funeral is in a few days.

Couldn't you leave and then come back? Have a break.

You're scrambling now, digging yourself deeper.

Obviously I can't leave him here.

For the first time since you have known her, you don't want to trade places. You have always regarded Ella's emotional literacy as the ultimate strength but seeing her like this, exhausted and unravelling, you are aware of something that you have been missing; that she views it as a burden. You say, of course, I'm sorry, and lurch forward to give her a hug. She reciprocates, wrapping her arms around you, but it feels forced. You wish that there was a script or template to follow on how to give comfort to someone, a guarantee that what-ever you said or did would be met with a positive reaction. She pulls back after a few seconds and continues making tea. You go to the bathroom and stay there for a long time.

The next morning you announce that you are going to the supermarket to replenish the fridge, expecting to be met with praise, but Ian and Ella barely look up from the TV when you leave. You are so relieved to be out of the stifling house that when the cold air hits your cheeks you sigh out loud.

You walk to the nearest Asda without tracking your route on maps, hoping that you'll get lost and kill some time before you have to go back to the house. You cross a white bridge stained with rust and wander along a path that runs beside a shallow river. It's drizzling and the sky is grey, the same colour as the rushing water, and the lack of light makes it feel like your vision has been filtered into black and white. There are a couple of boys clustered around a bench, wear-ing puffer jackets with their hoods up, and when you pass by them you smell weed. You have an urge to ask them for a draw, to hang around for a while, and immediately feel disgusted by yourself. Are these your peers? Teenagers who have nothing better to do than stand in the rain getting high and listening to trap remixes. You remember doing things like this when you were younger, hanging around local super-markets and parks, hoping that someone's older brother or boyfriend would buy you tins or cigarettes, longing for the day when you would be old enough to have something to do. You thought that turning eighteen would solve every-thing, that being in possession of a valid ID would be the only talisman you needed to have an exciting life, a life in which you possessed power and intrigue and the ability to get served. These days, you miss the agonies of being young; you would go back there in a heartbeat to escape the realities of adulthood. You would give away the agency that you longed for and wrote about endlessly in your diary for stagnancy, for rules.

You find the supermarket after half an hour, sandwiched between a carvery and a chain coffee shop. Looking in the windows of both, you see families and groups of friends eating and drinking coffee and it makes you feel so depressed you catch your breath. Not because you're lonely, on the contrary, you feel repelled by the bad lighting, the unself-conscious enjoyment, the sticky tables and greasy food. You wonder if Ella has ever come here with her family. You wonder if they had a good time. You are the same as your own parents in this respect, your revulsion at the thought of joining in, of playing the part of a happy family. There is something inside of you that finds it deeply embarrassing to enjoy things; to admit to enjoying things. You are so unlike Ella; a person who cries easily and openly and listens to uncool music without a hint of irony. You have never done anything without worrying that it's wrong. It's why almost nobody knows that you are ill, why your body feels like something you hide from and something to be hidden from others at the same time. It's why you are twenty-six and have no idea what you enjoy or feel passionate about, it's why you are a writer that does not write. When you were a teenager, you knew for certain that going out was cool; drinking and smoking and taking stuff, but now you have been shown time and time again that you are not made for it, that you cannot do these things without fucking up your own life and hurting other people. When you go inside the supermarket, you walk up and down the aisles, a headache forming behind your eyes from the strip lighting. Your basket is empty, you have no idea what Ian likes to eat. In the end, you fill the basket with food that you and Ella subsisted on in uni, pesto pasta, frozen pizzas, mountains of unhealthy snacks. You pause next to the fridge full of white wine, considering the pros and cons of adding alcohol into your already fraught situation. You end up throwing a few bottles of cheap Sauvignon Blanc into your basket, like you always do. When the cashier rings up your items, you grit your teeth at the price. You put the shop on your card, and your shoulders relax when the small screen flashes 'approved'.

Later, you and Ella are watching *Gilmore Girls* on the small TV in the living room. Ian was distracted during dinner and went to bed early. You watched Ella watching him as he left the room. You both listened to his thudding feet climb the stairs, heard a door open and close. Without speaking, Ella went to fetch the wine. You are filling yourself with salt and carbs, stodgy food that makes you lethargic. You feel like you are melting into the sofa, insides congealing like old soup and eyes drooping from the wine and the heat. Rory is sleeping with Dean on the TV, even though she knows he has a wife. Ella hates this bit. She is using a crisp as a vehicle for a small mountain of hummus without moving her eyes from the screen. The act is skilful, practised, until the very last moment when the crisp breaks apart, leaving jagged edges poking out of the dip like shark fins. She fishes the shards of crisp out of the bowl with her pointer finger and licks the hummus off. You say, gross, and she ignores you and says,

How old were we when this series came out?

You shrug, but she still isn't looking.

We were kids. We didn't watch it when it first aired.

You had watched it for the first time at uni with Ella, but you knew she had already seen it with another friend. You watch her dip another crisp into the hummus. It doesn't fall apart this time. She makes a face at the screen. Rory is fighting with her mother about Dean.

I just don't know how anyone could think that's okay. He's married. Fuck Rory.

I mean, fuck Dean more, right?

Ella puts her wine glass down a little too hard.

I don't care about Dean. He's stupid. It's Rory's fault.

You don't know if you agree with this.

I don't know if I agree with that.

Ella looks at you now, and you can tell she's annoyed. You aren't sure if it's with you or the show.

What do you think then? Do you think I'm being misogynistic?

You are too full of salt to think. You wait a few seconds, to make sure it isn't a rhetorical question. You decide to be honest.

I don't know what I think. Sometimes I think I just copy other people's opinions. Like I pretend to be angry if they are. I don't think I have much morality. I don't blame Rory.

She is definitely angry with you.

She knows he's married. Would you have got with the tutor if you knew he was married?

You sit up now.

Fuck. I don't know. I mean, I didn't know.

She narrows her eyes. You haven't seen her like this before, petty, trying to make you bite.

You would have, wouldn't you? That makes me so depressed. Like, I don't even know what to say to you.

I know. I'm hopeless.

She scoffs.

What does that mean? You're so passive. Things don't just happen to you.

Why are you so pissed off with me? I'm not her.

You point at the screen, but Ella doesn't react. You watch her pick nail varnish off her fingers and let the black bits fall onto the sofa. She notices you looking and stops.

Why are you here?

What do you mean? You asked me to come.

No, I didn't. Will did.

She pauses the TV and looks at you. Her eyes are hard, she doesn't even look like Ella.

I came because I wanted to help you.

She laughs.

That's funny.

I don't think so.

When she starts speaking, her voice is quiet, measured, but it feels like she's yelling.

You have never helped me or been there for me when I've been having a hard time.

You try to interrupt but Ella keeps talking.

You think nothing bad has ever happened to me.

You try to stop your voice from wobbling.

That isn't true. Remember Douglas? We went away. I tried to—

Ella raises a hand.

I booked that holiday. I sorted everything. You let me get drunk and do all that stuff with those boys. With you. Do you think that was good for me?

I was trying to help. I didn't know how to help you.

She sits up and gestures at you and then back at herself.

That's it, that's the problem! You never know how to do *anything*. I have to sort things out for you constantly. You do something insane and then you look at me with big fucking eyes like 'Ella fix it please' and then I *do* and then we move on and you don't even say thank you or care about how it makes me feel.

She is almost shouting now, and you have to hold back from telling her to be quiet in case Ian hears. It feels like you don't have the language to fix this, that everything you say is stupid and meaningless.

I'm really sorry you feel like that.

You're almost whispering, looking at the floor. Ella takes a deep breath and the next time she speaks it's like her anger has evaporated. Her voice is flat.

That apology doesn't mean anything. I don't 'feel' like that, it's the truth. It is exhausting being your friend. I feel like you take things from me, and I never get to be the one who needs support. You owe my *parents* money. I'm so done with it.

Done with me?

You are afraid of her; you feel like she is detaching from you. You remember when you walked in on her fighting with Douglas, and she was crying and surrounded by glass. Now, her eyes are dry. She stands up and says,

Yeah. I can't do it.

When she goes upstairs you don't follow.

You sit in the living room staring at the crisp bowl. You are supposed to be sharing a bed with her again tonight, sleeping in the sheets that Will slept in only a few days before. You are supposed to be making breakfast tomorrow and helping her to make food for the funeral. You check your phone and it's past midnight, there are no trains until morning, so you tidy up the living room on autopilot, washing the bowls and plates from dinner and rinsing the wine glasses. When everything is put away, you lie back on the sofa and try to fall asleep. You unpause the TV and let the rest of the episode play to fill the silence, staring at the screen as the closing sequence plays, then the title song for the next episode. By morning, the conflict between Rory and Lorelai has been fixed and all the characters have moved on. You get a bus to the station and put a ticket back to Glasgow on your card, stretching your overdraft even further. It occurs to you halfway through the journey that you can't go back to the flat, and you burst into tears, giving the man sitting opposite you such a fright that he spills his coffee. You apologise and he says it's fine and asks if you are okay and you say yes, even though you are still sobbing and there's snot all over your face. You go and stand in the empty space between carriages, next to the toilet, and, after some scrolling, you call Rowan. When he picks up, he says your name in a worried voice and you can't stop crying long enough to answer. He says, wait slow down it's okay. Tell me what's happened, and you manage to choke out, I haven't got anywhere to go.

Edinburgh

Rowan finds you a flat within days and arranges for your belongings to be packed up and moved to Edinburgh. He transfers you the money to pay Ian and Christine the rent you owe them, and helps you craft an email informing them that you are moving out. You send it to them the day after Ian's mother's funeral and receive a formal reply, terminating your lease, a few days later. You sign a rent contract for six months with a couple Rowan is friends with and pick up the keys from a neighbour. The only thing you know about Claire and Sam when you move into their home is their first names and the details of their bank account. The rent is suspiciously cheap for Edinburgh, so you expect that Rowan has called in a favour, or maybe told them about your situation to make them take pity on you. When you move into the flat, which only takes a few hours due to your meagre number of possessions, there's a note on the kitchen counter. It says – *feed Luna, keep the plants alive & make yourself at home. Claire x*

The cat is stretched out on the wooden floor of the kitchen in a ray of light and when you cautiously reach out to rub her warm belly, she meows sweetly and stretches her paws towards the watery sun.

The flat is beautiful, tastefully decorated and clean. You poke around the rooms, looking for clues about Claire and Sam's personalities and perversions, but can't find anything that hints at a dark side or anything less than domestic bliss. The books lining the shelves are immaculate, spines unbroken, mostly contemporary fiction and travel guides. There are fresh pink flowers in a glass vase on the coffee table, but you aren't sure what they're called. You text Rowan a photo and he replies: Carnations! Beautiful. Winter blooming and you smile as you read the message. You open all the cupboards, which are full of glass jars; lentils and pulses, neatly labelled spices; cinnamon sticks and real vanilla pods. You go into the bedroom, your bedroom, smooth your hand across the white duvet cover and fiddle with the radio on the bedside table, which is self-consciously retro and a chic shade of brown. This is the kind of place you daydreamed about living in with Rowan in the brief pockets of time since the abortion where you have allowed yourself to imagine a life together. It feels right that you are staying somewhere like this as a guest, the perfection a constant reminder that this way of living will always be temporary for you. It almost scares you how comfortable you are sitting here, surrounded by beauty, texting Rowan questions about flowers with no intention of ever telling him what he lost, what you took from him. It feels good that you are able to recognise the cruelty you are capable of. Rowan was unaware of this part of you for a long time, and you wonder if that's why you loved him so much and still romanticise the early days of your relationship. If you hadn't shown him your illness, your commitment to self-annihilation, maybe you could have stayed with him forever, pretending. You imagine the owners decorating when they first moved in. In your fantasy, Claire is eager to get started, rolling up her sleeves and dunking brushes into pots of glossy paint. Sam is more cautious, gentle, but he is willing to submit to his wife to ensure harmony. You wonder if this is true or if they bickered over what colour to paint the living room and agonised over the bathroom tiles.

The flat feels like an expression of their love for each other; the black and white wedding photo showing a tall blonde Claire and self-conscious but smiling Sam cutting a cake, the shelf of records preserved in plastic wrapping, the bottles of red wine in a wooden rack by the fridge. Everything is consciously collated, just enough colour and clutter to prevent the space from seeming sterile. You wonder why they left, and pause for a moment, trying to make up something that fits. You decide that they saved up to go travelling, collected trinkets to bring home and place on the shelves, learned how to cook new 'exotic' dishes to impress their dinner party guests. You text Rowan and say why did they want to sublet? and he replies immediately Divorcing. You cannot put into words how sad this makes you, and when a few minutes pass without your reply, he texts again: Are you okay? And you send him a photo of the wine rack: deciding where to start. He replies, Ha ha, and you can feel his disapproval through the screen.

You go out to explore your new neighbourhood before it gets dark. There's an independent coffee shop on the corner of the street and you peek inside, watching a handsome barista stack chairs in the corner while a few people finish up their drinks. The dim lights and soft furnishings make the small room look warm and inviting, and you imagine the sound of low chatter and clinking cups. You decide that this place will become your regular, somewhere you stop in for a flat white and a chat in the mornings before work. You touch your cheek with one hand, and it feels tight with cold. You need a scarf, some new knitwear, maybe a pair of winter boots. You want to fit in with the people inside, who are cool in a way you have never aspired to before; put together but still arty, understated in well-worn clothes that look expensive and comfortable. You still think of yourself as a student, but these people are all grown up. A woman sitting in the window looks up from her laptop and notices you peering inside. She smiles vaguely and picks up her tea with both hands, bringing it to her mouth to drink. You can feel the warmth of the cup under your own fingers.

A few weeks pass but you don't unpack. The boxes you brought with you remain untouched in the spare bedroom, which you rarely go into. Your IKEA photo frames, and holey sweatshirts stay packed away where you don't have to think about them. Instead, you eat off the matching plates and crockery that you find in the kitchen cabinets and use the sweet-smelling toiletries on the side of the bath. After a few days in the flat, you start wearing some of Claire's winter clothes. You know that this is crossing an unspoken line, but you can't stop yourself, and her cashmere socks and thick wool jumpers make you feel like a version of yourself that has been out of reach until now.

You have been bleeding steadily for over a month. This has happened before, but your attitude towards managing your health thus far has been to leave your body to its own devices, ignore the symptoms until they go away, and when you can't, numb yourself with whatever you have to hand. You want to break this habit, to become someone who treats themself and others well. You think about what Rowan would do, or Ella, and decide to call your GP and ask him to refer you to a gynaecologist in Edinburgh. On the morning of your appointment, you leak through your pad in the night and wonder if it's a bad omen. The blood is thick and muddy. The new gynaecologist, Dr Simpson, is quiet and neat and tucks her hair behind her ears compulsively. She asks you to tell her about your periods, starting from the beginning. You say, it's in my file, isn't it? You are tense, clutching your bag to your chest and ready to run. She swivels the computer screen around to face you to show you your records, and there it is, the evidence of your illness. Prescribed contraceptive pill for heavy periods, prescribed painkillers for period pain, referred to gynaecologist for ultrasound, ultrasound results normal, fitted for the hormonal coil, diagnostic laparoscopic surgery, diagnosed with endometriosis of the pelvis and appendix, appendix removed, partially expelled coil, first trimester abortion at home, and on and on it goes. It's hard to believe that in between the lines of text on the screen, you have been living a life. Or have you? Maybe this document tells Dr Simpson all there is to know about you. Maybe these are the defining facts of your life. She tucks her hair behind her ears again and leans forward, waiting for you to speak.

You are a child in a classroom; your primary school teacher is sending the boys into the dining hall and teaching the girls about the menstrual cycle. You are scoffing in disbelief at the tale that is being spun, at her insistence that there is a curving V inside you that is going to wake up one day and bleed, that this event will make you a woman. You are a teenager trying to swallow the threat of staining everything you sit on. You are learning how to hover above chairs barely touching the seat, every muscle in your body coiled as if you can prevent the blood from spilling out of you through willpower alone. You do not relax. You change pads between every class, in break and at lunchtime, but sometimes you touch your hand to the back of your skirt, and it comes away sticky. Your mother thinks you are lazy, dirty, and questions your inadequacy at using tampons, scolds you for the constant washing of sheets and skirts and underwear. You are skipping school when your period comes, waiting for your parents to leave for work and then slipping in through the back door and spending all day on the sofa watching panel shows and falling asleep with the lights on. You are fifteen and your mum stops getting periods altogether. You are jealous. You google how to get rid of your own period and you find alien words: hysterectomy, double ovariectomy, menopause. This will fix you. You pluck up the courage to ask your mother to go to the doctors; you tell her about the skiving, the anxiety that lives inside of you for three weeks every month, only to be realised when you wake up to bloodshed. She nods, and you are taken to the doctor to be put on contraceptives. You learn the spell of running the packets together. You cry when you pick up the prescription. Your mum is ashamed of this, your tears in the local pharmacy, your weakness.

You are surprised at how clearly you recall these feelings. That as soon as you start telling Dr Simpson about your medical history, memories rise to the front of your mind as clearly as if you were looking through photographs. You find it harder to remember the closer you get to the present, and you can barely conjure up the A&E visit in Belgium with Bertie, you can hear soft French voices and slamming doors and not much else. After you tell her about the final hospital trip, waking up without the coil and being sent home with the painkillers that blurred your existence, you stutter to a halt halfway through a sentence,

And then, you know what happened next.

Yes, I do.

She hands you a box of tissues and you realise that you have been crying for some time. Dr Simpson waits for you to blow your nose and pat your face dry and then she says,

I'm sorry all of this has happened to you.

She glances to the screen and back, then keeps talking.

What I'm noticing here is a consistent failure of pain management and support. These,

She points to the screen,

tell me the facts of your endometriosis, but I needed to hear from you how you've been feeling, how it has affected your life.

You take a breath and when you reply your voice is shaking,

It feels like it has been my whole life, sometimes.

She nods.

I can understand that.

She prescribes you the contraceptive pill again, the same one that you were on for years, an iron supplement to help replace some of the nutrients you are losing, and then a starter dose of antidepressants. She reminds you that a lot of people who have endometriosis find regulating their emotions difficult. It can cause dark moods. She asks if you can relate to that, and you feel like laughing. When you step outside, you notice you are crying again. You are going to take these tablets at the same time every day, with food. You are going to set an alarm, so you don't forget. You are going to go to bed earlier, wrap up warmer, eat better, do everything you can to help them to work. You have a purpose. You know Rowan would be happy to hear this from you, would be interested in your medication plan and impressed with the new doctor. You cannot bring yourself to phone him, to admit that you have finally followed his advice and you feel better for it. You've never liked doing things that are good for you, but maybe you can rewire yourself.

The next day, you go into the coffee shop and ask the barista if they're hiring. He shakes his head. You've been here a few times since you first passed, but every time you came in with big plans to stay for an afternoon and write, you ended up leaving after your first coffee. You felt self-consciously posed, sitting in the window as if on display. Everything about you felt wrong, your DIY fringe, your muddy trainers, the provocative stickers on your laptop that you thought were cool back in uni, but now seem childish. You had to psych yourself up to come and ask about jobs in the first place, and now you're here you want nothing more than to go back to the flat. You spend most of your time there, reading on the window seat or draining the bar cart, when you aren't wandering the city hoping to stumble upon a new job that will be different from the others. You want to do something that will enrich and excite you and pay you enough that you can start really living, so you can buy your own beautiful things. You don't have the energy to fill out another application, to edit your CV and try and convince someone in an expensive suit that you have good teamwork skills and an engaging personality. All the entry level jobs that you are qualified for seem to be focused on social media or brand management, and you still aren't convinced you know what the cloud is. You want to do something good, something small, something that makes you feel like a real person. You tell Rowan this on the phone late one night and he sighs, and you know that he's pressing his pointer finger to the crease between his eyebrows, like he always does when he's anxious or stressed. After a few seconds, he speaks.

I wish you would let me help you pay for a master's.

It's your turn to sigh now, angry instead of concerned.

I can't afford to do a master's, and there's no way I'll get funding. And I don't even know if I want to do it anymore.

I can help with the money, though.

I can't let you do that for me. It's too much.

The line is silent for a few seconds, and you feel like you can hear his brain whirring, trying to think of something to say that won't offend you. In the end, he settles on,

I know you think so, but I want to.

You feel so close to him when he's on the phone, his low, quiet voice in your ear. You can see him so clearly. When you ring him, it's always dark – you have an unspoken rule that you never talk on the phone during the day – and you close your eyes when he speaks, so you can concentrate fully on picturing him pacing back and forth in his study or watering the plants in the kitchen. It's easier to talk to him when he isn't in the same room.

Sometimes, you go all day without speaking to anybody at all, and on these days, you count down the minutes until the sun sets and you can call. He always picks up on the second or third ring and says, hi there, in a happy voice, like a sitcom dad. Sometimes when you say hi back, your voice rasps with disuse, and he asks you if you have a cold. You don't want him to know that you're lonely. Even at times like this, when he's annoying you, you feel like he's the only person left in the world who cares about you. Sometimes, you touch yourself while he tells you the minutiae of his day, a problem at work or a frustrating student. You suspect that he knows that you are doing this, that maybe he does the same when you recount your own thoughts, but you don't bring it up, so he doesn't either. This line connecting you is fragile and temporary, and neither of you want to stretch it too far in case it breaks.

The phone calls always end the same way, with you apologising for calling so often and Rowan reassuring you that he likes it, that he misses you and likes hearing your voice. Sometimes he tries to make plans to come and visit and you put him off, unwilling to deal with the awkwardness that would come with the inevitable discussion of sleeping arrangements, of defining your relationship. You want to touch him again, but you want it to be simple, like at the beginning when you didn't know each other. You know this is impossible, that too much has happened, but when you're talking on the phone, you forget. It would be harder to ignore if he was with you physically, lying next to you in bed or making eggs in the kitchen. You would have to be honest; there would be no escaping it.

Rowan was the one who suggested that you ask if the café was hiring. When the barista rejects you, you instantly begin to dread your next phone call, when Rowan will ask you what happened, and you will have to shoulder the burden of his disappointment. You order a coffee anyway and sit at an empty table in the corner of the café. It's busy, it's always busy, and you feel awkward about sitting at a table for three when you're alone. You prepare in your head what to say if someone comes over and asks to borrow a chair. *Yeah! Sure. Of course, you can.* You can feel your cheeks reddening at the shame of this charade. Now you're trying to live without Ella, it has become clear that her friendship was the only thing preventing you from becoming a total freak, someone who can't conduct themself in even the simplest of social situations. You pick at the edge of a sticker on your laptop that says THE FUTURE IS QUEER and try and peel it off in a single clean motion. Your nails aren't sharp enough to get purchase and it comes away raggedly, ripping and leaving half of the sticker on the back of the computer. Now it says IS QUEER, and THE FUTURE is curling in your palm. You drop it into your bag and give up. You are convinced that everyone in the shop heard your conversation with the barista, and now they either pity you or think that you're stupid for asking about jobs in the first place. The barista brings your coffee over, and your thank you comes out too abruptly, like you're being rude, and he frowns before he walks back to the counter.

By the time your coffee is half drunk, you are fantasising about returning home to bed. You are just about to pick your bag up off the floor and close your laptop screen when some-one taps you on the shoulder. You turn around and a woman with a pram asks you if she can sit with you because there aren't any other tables free. You nod and she puts the brake on the pram before sitting down heavily in the seat opposite, sighing and pushing her damp hair away from her face. She lets her head rest against the wall for a second and yawns. She's around your age, maybe a few years older, but there are circles under her eyes and lines on her forehead. Her buttons are done up wrong so you can see her black bra through the gaps in her shirt. You avert your eyes, so she doesn't catch you looking. She says,

Thank you, I'm Ivy.

And you nod and look at the pram. The hood is pulled low, so you can see the baby's chubby legs and feet poking out of the bottom of the seat. Ivy follows your gaze and speaks again,

She's asleep, finally.

Before the words have fully left her mouth, the baby starts to wake up. Her feet wriggle around, and you can hear her breathing change. Ivy looks panicked.

She always falls asleep when I walk around, but I'm knackered. I needed to sit down.

She starts to move the pram back and forth in jerky motions.

What's her name?

You ask, because you can't think of anything else to say.

Gracie. She's one.

You nod. The barista comes back over and Ivy smiles at him and says hello.

Can I get you ladies anything else?

Yes, please Alex. Can I have a long black? And the soup.

She turns to you,

And do you want anything? I'll buy you a coffee for letting me invade your table.

You shake your head, but she insists, so you concede. When Alex leaves, it is quiet again, except for Gracie's snuffles. A man enters the café, talking loudly on his phone, and Gracie wakes up properly and starts to scream. Ivy sighs, pulls the hood back and undoes a series of complicated connecting straps, freeing Gracie. You look at her, and she looks back at you and instantly stops shouting. Tears keep spilling out of her brown eyes and her lip keeps shaking, but she's quiet. You smile, awkwardly, and give her a little wave. Gracie clenches and unclenches her fist, like she's trying to wave back. Ivy laughs.

She likes you!

You never know what to say when people tell you that their baby likes you. You aren't sure if you should say thank you. You tap Gracie's knee and say, I like your dungarees, and she looks at you, bored. Ivy is smiling.

She's very judgemental. Don't worry. She looks at me like that all the time.

You find this funny, the implication that this tiny baby has a personality. You don't know any babies well, and they have only ever functioned as a disturbance in your life; an interruption to a conversation, a reason for parents to leave parties early or not come at all. Watching Rowan with his friend's baby, whose name you have forgotten, you felt moved, but in a selfish way. The idea of him being a father turned you on and also excited you as a way to prove his commitment and love to you. The baby, in both cases, was irrelevant. You are aware that this outlook on children is juvenile, and something that you will be expected to grow out of. You decide to make yourself interested in Gracie, to cosplay as a normal heterosexual woman and ask questions that are expected of you.

Can I hold her?

You blurt out, and Ivy looks taken aback, and then grateful.

Of course. That would be good actually. It's been a while since I got to eat a meal with both hands.

Gracie is deposited on your lap and instantly, mechanically, reaches both hands out for her mother. You pick her up to return her to Ivy and she shakes her head.

No, it's fine. She'll get over it.

You turn Gracie to face you and try to think of ways to be entertaining. She still looks bored, like she's ready to resume crying at any moment. You feel too self-conscious to do the things that you have seen other women do to engage babies, singing or shouting in a jolly, manic voice. Gracie holds up a chubby hand and pulls a clump of your hair, quite hard. You say, ow, automatically, and then she laughs. You feel a sense of achievement, and tug one of her ponytails, gently, making your face mock outraged. Gracie laughs again and you begin to understand her appeal. She is very cute, objectively, her round pink cheeks and black hair in spiky little bunches. You lift her up a little, so she can straighten her legs and stand assisted on your lap. Ivy is shovelling soup into her mouth and says, her mouth full, she likes walking around. You stand up, holding her as carefully as possible, surprised by the weight of her, how substantial and human she feels. You walk her over to a tall monstera plant in the corner of the shop and show her the leaves. You say, see, look, they're kind of shiny, and Gracie solemnly reaches out to touch a leaf. She looks back at you, her eyes bright, and you feel like she understands you, like you are engaged in a complex secret language comprised of eye contact, facial expressions, and telepathic communication. You take her up to the counter and point at the cakes behind the glass screen, telling her what each one is and how much they are. She touches the glass in front of a caramel brownie, leaving behind a perfect fingerprint smudge, and you say, look how little your fingers are compared to mine, and touch the pad of your thumb against her own. You notice that the barista, Alex, is watching you, amused, but you don't feel embarrassed. You would never have had the confidence to go and peruse the cakes on your own, but with Gracie, your little mate, you feel like you have a sense of purpose. You look back at Ivy and say, can I get her a cake? and Ivy gives you a thumbs up. You order the brownie, and when you pay, you let Gracie hold a pound coin, which she looks at with wonder before depositing it neatly in her mouth. You look back at Ivy, panicked, but she's on her phone, so you prise open Gracie's mouth and take the money out, which isn't as difficult as you thought it would be, and when it looks like she's about to cry, you remind her of the brownie in a calm voice and she relaxes. Your heart is still beating fast as you walk her back to the table, images of Gracie choking and being rushed to hospital blooming in your mind. You tell Ivy, the words rushing out in a jumble.

She put some money in her mouth but she's ok, I got it out and she seems fine.

Ivy nods and takes Gracie back, giving her a quick cuddle and assessing her expression for signs of distress.

She always does that. It's fine, well done for noticing and sorting it out.

You glow from the praise. You wish Rowan could have seen you, capable of assessing and rectifying the situation. You know it would have made him happy. Alex brings the brownie over and Ivy cuts off a small piece for Gracie and splits the rest between you.

She's not really allowed sugar, but I let her have the odd bit of chocolate.

You apologise, saying you didn't realise that she was too wee, and Ivy shakes her head, and says it's fine, that the two of you can share the rest. When it's time for them to leave, you feel a tug of fear at the prospect of not seeing them again. You ask Ivy for her phone number and suggest maybe

173

going for a coffee. You tell her you live nearby and you're new to the area. She writes her phone number on a napkin and signs it with a heart. When you walk home, you realise that a few hours have passed without you worrying about jobs or thinking about Ella. You arrive back at the flat with a feeling of purpose, and when you take your tablets and go to bed, you fall asleep almost instantly.

The next night, you are up in the early hours, talking to Rowan on the phone about poetry. You have the thought, once again, that he is more real to you in these conversations than he ever was when you were together. You find it easy to separate the Rowan whose child you lost from the Rowan who is talking to you now, asking questions about structure and tone. He's quiet for a moment, you hear rustling and then he speaks,

Sorry I'm eating. So, what were you saying? You mean that you don't think you ever want to write your own stuff?

I don't think so, no. I don't think I have the temperament for it.

What do you mean?

I think you have to be good at talking about your feelings to be a poet.

He laughs.

Okay. Don't love that you laughed at that.

You can tell that he's smiling when he replies,

Sorry, sorry. Rude of me. Isn't that how you work out how you feel though, writing it down? That's how I feel about my journal.

You smile.

Yeah I know you love your journal.

You are very sarcastic on the phone, did you know that?

You make a non-committal noise and he laughs again.

I would just love to read your poetry. I feel like it would be so wonderful. And it would be a nice way to get back into thinking about poems, and then maybe leading on from that, academia?

You knew this was coming.

Oh here we go. I feel like I'm being scolded.

You are! It is baffling to me. I want to support your career, but you don't even want to talk about the future. You have all of this talent stored up in your head but it's like you're putting off really getting started. What is stopping you from just going back into a master's? I'll pay. I just want you to do it.

His faith in you used to make you feel good, but now you just feel sorry for him, for how effectively you have him fooled.

It's funny that you say I have talent. Like you have any proof of that. I can't just start. It's like my wisdom tooth that's coming through. I'm trying to forget about writing, because I have so much other stuff I'm supposed to be doing, but it keeps bothering me. The idea won't leave me alone.

Rowan is silent for a second, and you can tell he's going to change the subject.

I can't believe you still haven't got your wisdom teeth checked. It's been years.

You roll your eyes, before you remember he can't see you.

You're scolding again.

I know. But you should go to the dentist.

I have no money. It'll figure itself out.

It will not. If it hurts it needs to come out. Also, I feel worried when you say things like that to me. That you have no money.

You try to interrupt but he talks over you.

No, let me say this. I know you don't want me to help, but I want to do things for you. I want to help you. I'm sorry if that embarrasses you.

You smile.

It doesn't embarrass me; it makes me feel cared about.

That's good.

You're both silent. You reach this impasse in your conversations all the time. Him expressing his desire to do things for you and improve your life, usually through financial aid, you gently knocking him back. After these phone calls, usually the next morning, money will appear in your bank account. You wish you had the strength to send it back, but every time you spend it and hate yourself. Neither of you address the transactions explicitly, and sometimes it feels like he is paying you for the phone calls, paying you to stay in his life. It forces you to acknowledge that although Rowan is incredibly precious to you, his presence is also unsustainable; that maybe his unsustainability is why he is precious in the first place. You can't figure out who holds the power in the relationship anymore, who has the ability to break whose heart. By virtue of Rowan's age, wealth and general maturity in comparison to yours; an aimless drifter with a maxed-out overdraft and no friends, it should be him. But there are other things at play; your secrets, your youth and what it represents, the glaring fact that you broke up with him. If you're honest with yourself, you can reach the conclusion that you are probably going to hurt him soon, and badly, even worse than you did when you left him the first time. Acknowledging that fact doesn't feel like winning, but it does make you feel secure.

You wait three long days to text Ivy. You are eager to see Gracie again, to regain the competence you felt when you were holding her and walking around the shop, trusted to keep her safe and procure brownies for her at will. You agonise over the composition of the text, drafting and redrafting to convey an air of breeziness through your language. In the end you write, so good to meet you the other day. Would love to have a coffee/brownie with you and gracie again soon x Ivy's reply is immediate and riddled with typos and exclamation marks. She asks what you're doing this afternoon and invites you round to her flat. You appreciate the urgency of her invitation because it doesn't allow time for you to overthink your outfit and general appearance. Her flat is difficult to find, and you wander up and down side streets in the drizzle, close to giving up before you finally stumble upon her building. When she buzzes you in your hair is damp and frizzy. Ivy opens the door and hugs you tightly before you can catch your breath, and although you are not usually a hug person, you force yourself to return the embrace, and after a second, it feels good. She apologises for not meeting you outside, explaining that Gracie has a cold and has been asleep most of the morning. You try to hide your disappointment that Gracie will most likely not be a part of your day and feel nervous at the prospect of spending time with Ivy without the buffer of the baby. She leads you into a kitchen-living room area and encourages you to make yourself comfortable while she checks on Gracie. You find this difficult because every available surface is covered with things. There are piles of books on the kitchen table, clean laundry strewn across all visible chairs, and mugs and toys and bottles everywhere else that someone could possibly sit down. When Ivy comes back you are still hovering, and she apologises for the mess.

It's just me and Gracie here. I'm a freelancer, so I work from home. I wish I could say that the flat doesn't usually look like this, but I'd be lying.

That's ok, I understand.

Your past living spaces have always looked like this, and you have never had the excuse of a baby or a busy job. These days, the flat you live in is clean and tidy. The antidepressants make it easier for you to do small tasks, put away your dishes and washing. Without the constant bleeding you are sleeping better and waking up earlier. It feels small, but you want to tell Ella. You are starting to think that the things that have long made up your personality; messiness, disorganisation, lateness, are maybe not who you are at all. You can't believe other people have lived their whole lives like this, with all this time in the day to get coffee and walk around and fold their clothes. It occurs to you that you could give Ivy the impression that you have always been this way. Through her eyes you could become someone capable, someone that you like. You ask her what kind of freelancing she does, and she tells you she's a graphic designer and then your conversation stalls. Ivy swirls the coffee around in her cup and looks awkward.

I'm glad you texted actually. It feels random to ask but I need someone to look after Gracie. I was looking on child-care websites and stuff but the other day in the coffee shop felt serendipitous. I'm a big believer in that kind of thing, are you?

You aren't, but you agree. You're blindsided, not sure if you're allowed to be offended that Ivy doesn't want to be your friend when you had come to see Gracie anyway.

I've never done anything like that before.

Ivy looks relieved that you aren't annoyed and shakes her head roughly.

No, I know, I could tell. It's fine, I could help. She liked you and I liked you. I don't really want to be a proper boss, you know? I want somebody that I like.

You know that Ivy is flattering you but it's working. You blush and she keeps going.

I would need quite a lot of hours; I have a big project coming up. If you already had stuff going on—

You laugh.

I have nothing going on.

Ivy smiles and says that's good and asks you some questions about wages and hours and when you agree, she goes to fetch Gracie. You sit, surrounded by clutter, a little stunned. When Ivy comes back into the room, holding a pyjama-clad Gracie, you reach your arms out for her automatically. Ivy hesitates and you watch her hold her baby a little tighter.

Her dad isn't involved. I don't speak to my parents. We're on our own here.

You nod.

So am I.

You start by taking Gracie for two hours. Ivy confirms that you received her email outlining their usual routine and sends the two of you on your way within five minutes of your arrival; you with a heavy baby bag on your back and Gracie clutching a small orange fox. Blind leading the blind. Ivy doesn't like working in cafés, so you are pushed out into the world to pass the time. You can take her back to your flat, to a park, to a café, wherever. The freedom is too much to bear, and you find yourself asking Gracie what she wants to do, looking at her pouting face and wishing she could give you an answer. She is holding the fox, Mimi, so tightly by the neck that you have to fight the urge to take the toy away and save it. You push her back to the flat in her pram, conscious that you should maybe tell the owners that you are entertaining an infant in their perfect home. You text Rowan and say, i'm with Gracie. i don't know what to do. When you told him about the new job, he was silent and then happy. You know that this must be difficult for him, but he would never burden you with his sadness. He asks to see Gracie so you video call him, switching the camera to front facing so he can only see Gracie and you can only see him. He is smiling and he says, she's beautiful, and Gracie turns her head from side to side, wondering where the new voice is coming from. You show her his face on the phone, and she puts her face close to the screen, blurring the screen with her breath, trying to put it into her mouth. Rowan laughs and Gracie jerks her head away in surprise, then laughs herself. Rowan says, I wish I was there with you. We would have so much fun. After a minute he has to hang up, he's getting ready for a date, and you can tell that he's nervous. When you say goodbye, you try to get Gracie to wave unsuccessfully, and when you finally hang up, you're all laughing.

The day passes and you both survive. You learn that Gracie likes songs, that she can sing along with them using her gibberish language and hold a tune impressively well for a one-year-old. She can stand up and move a step or two before she falls backwards onto her bum and puts a fist in her mouth. She likes to stand up and dance to the music, bopping up and down while you hold her hands. She loves it when you make Mimi dance, and says her name over and over again like a chant, Mi-mi-mi-mi-mi. It's the only almost-word she knows. You make her lunch and snack without incident and return her to Ivy at 1pm. You pass the test and then, without ceremony, you are Gracie's nanny.

*   *   *

In your previous jobs, weekends were a period of time in which you lived your real life and followed your desires. You hoped to live well enough so that when Monday came around and you went back to work you felt like you had enough left-over happiness to last you until Friday. Now, without you noticing, weekends have become things to be endured until you can go to work and see Ivy and Gracie again. You torture yourself by wondering what they are doing on these days, whether they're in the park you take her to on Mondays, or at some weekend music class. Once, you glimpse them walking down the street together on a Sunday afternoon, Gracie asleep in her sling attached to Ivy's chest, and you feel such a strong pull towards the two of them that you have to turn around and walk quickly back to the flat. Your weekend plans become unimportant compared to your weekdays, where you have been tasked with protecting the safety and happiness of a real human being. Gracie becomes the most important person in your life within weeks, and you can tell that Ivy is surprised, and maybe a little suspicious of the intensity of your feelings.

You have Gracie for five or six hours every weekday and spend this time pushing her pram around parks while she sleeps, taking her to baby classes and cafés, making her healthy meals and playing with her in your flat. You feel more confident than you ever have. With the security of a baby strapped to your chest or resting on your hip, people are automatically kinder to you and treat you with more authority. You find it easy to ask for things to accommodate Gracie; a highchair or a babycino and you stop saying sorry all the time to everyone you meet. Men don't approach or catcall you when you are with her, and other women with buggies nod to you on the street and give you sympathetic looks when she cries. You let them think that she belongs to you. Around midday, you take her back to Ivy's so she can breastfeed, and you spend a happy half hour having a coffee from the nice machine and chatting to Ivy about books and her job, before taking Gracie back outside for her afternoon nap. You are paid well, a lot more than your old jobs bartending and serving coffee, and about the same as your old customer service job at the app. You notice things about Ivy's lifestyle that don't make sense, her expensive kitchen gadgets, tailored clothes, the mortgage on the flat and your paycheques. She has led you to believe that you are kindred spirits, women who are getting by on their own. She doesn't know about Rowan, who still calls you most nights and sends you money that you both pretend doesn't exist. You decide that you are both allowed to have secrets.

One morning, you are pushing Gracie on the swings and your underwear fills with blood. Dr Simpson warned you that it might take months for your periods to stop or get lighter, and that you should be prepared for irregularities in your cycle until then. You had woken up tearful and aching that morning and found Gracie annoying, and you feel relieved that you can put it down to this, that it isn't your fault that you have been irritated by her. You take Gracie to a coffee shop disabled bathroom because you are far away from your flat, and you sit her on the sticky floor while you try to clean up. She watches you silently as you change your underwear for the clean pair you keep in your bag and throw away the soiled pair. You feel embarrassed even though she doesn't know what you're doing. You want to take her back home to her mother and sleep for the rest of the day. This is why you should not have children. Gracie gets bored of sitting on the floor and reaches out for you, but you ignore her and put your head in your hands. She starts to cry, and you plug your ears with your fingers.

You are not supposed to be someone who thinks this way anymore, you are supposed to be new. Dr Simpson told you to disclose your condition to your next employer and discuss reasonable adjustments that would make it easier for you to be a good employee. She told you that endometriosis is classed as a chronic pain condition that can make it difficult to work, that you are not lazy, just sick. You ignored this advice, and now you are being punished. Someone knocks on the door, and you say, someone's in here, and Gracie keeps crying. Your trousers are still around your ankles, you are pathetic, and you want to stay here forever. You force yourself to look at Gracie's red face, which is soaked in real tears. You have navigated her frustrations and tantrums, but this time she is upset and afraid and it is your fault. You wash your hands and pick her up. You tell her that you're sorry, whisper it in her hair, but she is crying too loud to hear you. You pick up the bag and manage to balance Gracie against your hip and unlock the pram. She is screaming directly into your ear, making you feel off balance as you lurch out of the bathroom into the coffee shop. Everyone is looking at you and you force yourself to walk out of the café slowly and calmly. You get onto your knees and strap Gracie into the buggy, saying I'm sorry, I'm sorry, over and over. She doesn't hear you or doesn't care. She doesn't want a snack or water; she just wants to squeeze Mimi by the neck and cry. Once she is secured into the seat you start walking without planning a destination. Her screams don't seem as loud now you're out on the street next to the road, and you walk and walk steadily, avoiding bumps on the pavement until she falls asleep. You are too afraid to stop walking in case she starts crying again, so more than an hour passes without you sitting down. It occurs to you that your mother must have done things like this countless times when you were a child; kept going past the point of exhaustion, hurt herself trying to help you. You soften towards her, imagining her soothing you the way that you soothe Gracie. When she was crying in the toilet you felt a weariness that seemed like it came from something older than yourself, something built in. You think about calling your mum when you get home and telling her that you're a nanny, maybe asking her for advice. When Gracie wakes, you are in an area of Edinburgh that you have never come to before, and she looks around blinking, wondering where she is and rubbing sleep from the corners of her eyes.

Claire gets in touch with you to ask if you want to renew your lease and stay in the flat for another six months. You look around the flat while she waits for an answer, trying to ignore the boxes in the hallway that you still haven't unpacked. You've kept their things immaculate, washing and ironing Claire's clothes after you wear them, scrubbing the sink until it squeaks. Why can't you take care of your own things like this? You hear her sigh on the end of the phone.

Are you still there?

Yeah sorry. Can I call you back later today?

Sure.

It would be so easy to stay here until you were kicked out, never having to buy your own dishes or hang your clothes up in the wardrobe. You are surrounded by the aesthetic signi fiers of happiness, and you haven't had to earn any of them.

But you don't want to be here anymore. You know that you've been feeling this way for a while. It's easy to look after yourself here, do the things that Dr Simpson wants you to do. But it feels like cheating. You call Claire back and tell her that you're moving out.

You don't tell Rowan that you're looking for flats, because you know that if he offers to help then you'll let him. You find a room in a flat, sharing with four students. Your space is small, and when you move in, filthy, with a window that barely opens and damp on the ceiling, but you paid for it by yourself and after you clean and unpack, it looks fine. You take a moment to mourn the loss of Claire and Sam's coffee machine, but you try your best to romanticise the cafetière you find in the charity shop down the road. You put off sending Rowan pictures of your room, because you know he'd be appalled, but you are surprised by how nice it is to exist in a place that belongs to you instead of being a guest in somebody else's home.

Every Friday afternoon, Ivy asks if you have weekend plans, and you make something up, so she doesn't feel sorry for you. This time, you tell her that you have a date, and she says,

Oh, I was hoping you'd babysit.

You try and backtrack; say you'd be happy to take Gracie and cancel your plans, but Ivy waves her hand and says it's okay. You walk home from work, dreading another evening of making dinner and reading in bed while your flatmates get ready to go out. You can't believe how exhausting it is to keep yourself together every day, to cook nourishing meals, to walk outside and keep your room clean. You listen to a podcast about mindful drinking as you walk back to your flat and wonder if trying to like yourself will always be this hard, this constant.

One of your flatmates, Liv, is in the kitchen washing dishes when you get back, and you linger for a moment, trying to work up the nerve to speak. She jumps when she notices you and you apologise.

That's okay. How are you?

You tell her you told your boss you were going on a date.

Oh no way, with who?

I'm not actually going out. I just didn't want her to think I had no plans.

Liv laughs and wipes her wet hands on her thighs, dripping suds onto the floor. You fight the urge to pass her a towel and wonder if you are becoming your mother.

Why don't you come out with us?

You're flattered by the invitation but have no urge to accept. While you are trying to think of a polite way to say no, Liv speaks,

It's okay. I know you probably don't want to. We must seem so childish to you, so studenty. Just wanted you to know that you're welcome.

You don't seem childish. It isn't that. But thank you for asking.

Why don't you go on a date for real then?

You hadn't considered that. After a second Liv turns back to the dishes and you go to your room. You download a dating app onto your phone, one you haven't used before, and click the option that says you're interested in all genders. Making a profile is unbearable, scrolling through photos of yourself to find one that isn't horrific, wondering what kind of impression you want to make. There is no Ella to choose a picture or craft a witty first message, and you wonder if you will ever be able to think about her without feeling a pain in your chest.

You go out for margaritas with an art student called Maisie who has a quiet, musical voice and tiny tattoos all over her arms. You are attracted to her, but you still don't trust yourself completely. She tells you about growing up in the Highlands, you talk about Gracie too much, and you force yourself to switch to water after three drinks. When you get back to her place, you sit in the bedroom, and she switches the big light off. When she turns on her salt lamp, the room becomes soft and pink. She lights incense and laughs when she notices your face and gestures to her bookshelf, full of astrology books and thick volumes about witchcraft.

I know, I am a huge cliché. Do you think it's a load of rubbish?

You shake your head, smiling, thinking about the profiles you scrolled through earlier that evening; the men with bios detailing lists of deal-breakers when it came to women, or outlining their kinks and sexual preferences; which all seemed to involve hurting you in some way. You don't understand star charts and wicca and can't picture yourself being in a relationship with Maisie, but you feel safe here, breathing in the spiced scent, sitting on her comfortable sheets. You realise that you want to kiss her, and maybe hang out again, but that your expectations end there. You can recall a time, embarrassingly recently, when you would have changed the shape of yourself to accommodate her; made her interests your own, changed the way you dressed and spoke. You realise now that nobody has ever forced you to do this, that you made the decision to erase yourself all on your own. You can blame drugs, or alcohol, or sex, but you never had an issue with those things, not really. You have spent years using anything you can find to hurt yourself. When Maisie kisses you, you try to empty your mind of insecurities and worries, to focus on the pleasure. It feels good, everything just feels so good.

When you get back to the flat, it's quiet. The kitchen table is littered with the remnants of pre drinks; a full ashtray, assorted bottles of mixers and spirits, playing cards arranged in a fan around a plastic cup half-full of murky liquid. You wash and dry the glasses, bin the cigarette butts and wipe the sticky table, happy to busy yourself with a simple task. When you're finished, you look around the clean kitchen and think, what next? While you're getting changed, Maisie texts you asking if you're home safe, and you smile as you type out a reply, becoming aware of how much you have missed having somebody in the same city as you query your whereabouts. In bed, you open your book, but lose focus after a few pages. You are struck by the urge to write something, and when you open your laptop you find that you aren't wondering what to say, but simply, where to start.

i haven't called you because i'm bad at expressing my feelings in the moment and i tend to get defensive. i've been thinking about our fight constantly and you're right and i'm sorry. i want to apologise for everything – but how do you apologise for being a bad friend for eight years?

i always relied on my body to tell me how i felt because i didn't know how to figure out my own emotions. like, my throat felt tight, so i knew i was about to cry therefore i knew i was sad, that kind of thing. then i met you and i didn't have to do that anymore.

when you told me that I was exhausting to be friends with, i was surprised. i actually feel embarrassed writing that now, because i know that it's true. i always idolised you and believed that as long as you were in my life, it meant that i must be doing something right. it made sense for me to use you as a way to translate my own feelings. if I couldn't figure myself out, i'd ask you and you always knew. i realise now how much pressure that is to put on someone, especially the person i love the most. that feels strange to write because we never say it but i do love you. i know now that you never felt my love, you just felt my need. that must have been maddening.

the diagnosis felt like a sign, not from god or anything, i'm not insane, more like a confirmation that i was made wrong. it felt reassuring. i was vindicated knowing that there was something physically wrong with me. that I was separate from other people. i know that's self-absorbed.

i have been getting better since i moved out. i don't know if you know, but i live in edinburgh, i'm working, i'm seeing a doctor. i was living in a flat that belonged to rowan's friends but they came home so now i'm somewhere new, sharing with some students. it reminds me of being in halls, they remind me of us. my room is nice. i am starting to buy nice things for myself. i want to tell you about it, about everything i'm doing, but mostly i want to hear about you.

i wasn't there for you when your grandmother died, and a million other smaller times. you watched me blow up my life over and over again and i made you pick up the pieces. you watched me move on and barely think about the people i had hurt. i need you to know that it wasn't like that when i left wales. i have been thinking about you every second.

i want to be in your life in a way that isn't draining for you. i don't know how to do that yet and i'll probably fuck up loads but i am asking you anyway, even though i feel so vulnerable I want to die. mainly i am saying sorry – a real sorry. you don't have to reply.

Queen's Park

When her name appears in your inbox, you feel like you're going to be sick. You scan the email and pick up phrases like, it really fucking hurts my feelings when, and, you need to realise that this has been … You read it through once, quickly. Towards the end of the email her tone softens. You read, i want good things for you, and, going forward maybe we can, and you think, maybe it's okay. You read it again, and again. Instead of typing out a response, you pick up the phone and call her. The phone rings twice, three times, four, then she picks up.

You get the train to Glasgow to meet her. She's moved in with Will, her parents are selling the flat, and, just like that, the evidence of your life together is gone. You are sweating and dishevelled when you meet her, your hair won't go right, and you've been touching it so much it looks flat and greasy. She meets you at the entrance to the park and she's wearing a linen dress that you don't recognise. You thought that you had become immune to her beauty, that the longing feelings you once had for her had deepened into a love that was strictly platonic, but no, there's the ache in your stomach, the catch of your breath. You don't hug or touch each other, but she smiles and says hi, and gestures for you to walk into the park. You ask how she is, and she says yeah, really good. Are you good? And you check yourself before you answer, hold back from telling her about your long shift that morning, about Gracie's new words and your argument with your flatmate. You say that you're pretty good and she says, that's good, and you both laugh, an acknowledgement that this is strange. You walk past the ice cream van and watch the kids queue up for sweets. You notice a kid at the back of the line, clutching a five pound note in one fist. He's staring awestruck at the pictures on the side of the van showing 99s with flakes, flying saucers and fizzy belts. You point him out to Ella, and she looks at you bemused, shaking her head and smiling. She says that there's something different about you and it makes you feel self-conscious. You walk past the shallow pond dotted with swans and then deeper into the park. The trees shade your bodies, and you watch Ella rub her bare arms. You ask about the flat, about Will and she says,

I'm stupidly happy. He's good. The flat's amazing.

And you say that you'd love to see it. She says you can come round for a coffee at some point, if you want to, and you accept, shyly, like you're brand new to each other. You emerge from the trees into the sun, talking about nothing, and walk up the hill until you reach the flagpole. It's busy because of the weather, families are having picnics and groups of people are drinking and listening to music. You are tired, but good tired, your back aches from lifting Gracie and you didn't get enough sleep because you stayed up late reading. You could go back into town now, get the train home, pick up bits for dinner and catch up on your washing. You could ask Ella if she wants to buy wine and try to find a place to sit in the park. You are reaching an exit now, the one close to the station, and Ella turns to you expectantly. You ask if she's free now for a coffee and she nods like you've said the right thing. You're being cautious with each other, trying to start again but your shared history is still there, in the way you automatically shorten your stride to match hers, the way you both roll your eyes when a topless guy cycles past you playing music from a speaker. She leads the way back to her new flat, and you follow her, and everything is the same but different.

Author's Note

The average diagnosis time for endometriosis is 7.5 years from the onset of symptoms. It affects an estimated 1 in 10 people with a uterus in the UK and is the second most common gynaecological illness.

Acknowledgements

Thank you to my family: Mum, Dad, Geni, Stu, Jo, Gramma and Grampa. Without you, I wouldn't have any of this. Posy Mae, I can't wait for you to read this when you are eighteen.

Thank you to the team at John Murray, for falling in love with the book and for looking after me so well. Thank you, especially, to Abi – for getting it. I am lucky to have you as my editor.

To my agent, Stan, for fighting for *Gender Theory* from the very beginning and for explaining what everything means. Thanks for picking me.

To my uni tutors – Meghan Flaherty, Sophie Collins, Elizabeth Reeder, Gillian Shirreffs. Thank you for treating me like a writer when I didn't think I was one. Special thank you to Meg – the best email therapist money can't buy.

Many thanks to Trev and Robin for the use of their perfect cottage. And Trev – thank you for reading my work from the beginning.

I wouldn't have been able to write this book without talking to my friends, a lot. Somehow, those conversations turned into a book, and for that, I can't thank you all enough. Chris and Robin – thank you for your shed, the marg nights, the printer ink. Phoebe – thank you for letting me steal your anecdotes. Dom – thank you for forwarding that email, I owe you drinks forever. Ciara and Aisch – thank you for workshopping me, even though you don't have to anymore.

Matthew – It feels unoriginal to say thank you for everything. But thank you, truly, for everything. People are boring, but you're something else completely.